IF EVER I FALL

The Letter Club – Book 2

Elle Wright

PRAISE FOR THE LETTER CLUB

Nothing Else But You

"This was one of my favorites from an author period. It had everything I love in a novel. The characters and plot had me from beginning to end. Highly recommend." ~JuliaBookLandReviews

"I totally fell in love with this book, Gio is a dream and so is his girl. We get to know them through their letters and want them to get on in real life despite all the possible problems and obstacles. My new favourite author." ~JennyIndigo

"Wow! Loved it. I found the letters so great for a written style. The couple finding out about each other and falling in love without ever meeting. Awesome characters with so much emotion. A must read!" ~Laura Johnston

"This story was so touching. The plot is emotionally brilliant and the characters fit in perfectly. I love the emotional vulnerability and chemistry the protagonists have." ~PinkieIsShy

"Old fashioned letter writing has never been done better." ~Loni

www.BOROUGHSPUBLISHINGGROUP.com

IF EVER I FALL
Copyright © 2020 Elle Wright

ISBN 978-1-951055-48-6

When you're sure, don't ever give up

ACKNOWLEDGMENTS

To all the young women who know their minds, desires, wishes and dreams. Forge ahead, don't give in, give up, or let anyone tell you how to live your life. If you know it's right, you'll get there. The journey is part of the greatest ride life can offer. Hold on with both hands and go for it.

Thanks to my beta reader, aka Miss Honesty. 'Preciate you more than you know. To Boroughs Publishing Group, thank you for being there.

IF EVER I FALL

Di Caro Residence
Dutchford, Connecticut
Sofia

Hi number 980462. I'm sitting at my drafting table in my studio surrounded by sketchpads, pencils, pens, tools, my press, and wood blocks, which is why this is written on sketch paper. I find comfort here. It's one of the few places I can be where I get lost in my work and shut out the world. When I'm creating, everything else falls away and time becomes irrelevant. Sometimes the only reason I go to bed is because my nonna or my mom come get me. Right now I'm working on a piece that's larger than what I typically do. It's a landscape, also different for me, but it's a place etched into my brain, and you know why it will always be.

My life has become even smaller than it had been when I was in Sicily. Now I have no phone, and I'm not allowed to drive my car. I'm driven everywhere in a blacked-out SUV. When it pulls up to the school, I slink out and run inside. I'm embarrassed and humiliated. I can't live like this for much longer. The good news, I won't have to. Seven months and sixteen days until I graduate, and the same week I get out of high school, I turn eighteen. I won't have to live like a cloistered nun anymore.

Last night I went to four Halloween parties with Amy, Gio, and Nat. I couldn't believe my parents let me go. Gio said he didn't have to do any convincing, but I don't believe him. It seemed too normal, which means we were probably followed all night, and I didn't pick up the tail.

Anyway, the first three parties were at houses off campus that had like six or eight guys living in each house. Even though the houses were packed with wall-to-wall people, you could tell the places were a mess all the time. We didn't stay long at any of the houses. I think we stopped by so Gio could make an appearance. He didn't say, but I'm guessing some of his teammates lived in each place.

The best party was the one at a hotel downtown. The DJ was great, the costumes were outrageous, and the bathrooms were clean.

You'd be surprised how many girls rate places on how clean the bathrooms are. For real, I mark down restaurants if their bathrooms are only okay. If they're skank, I won't eat there again. I figure they keep the food and the kitchen as clean as they keep the bathroom.

I went as Carrie – the Sissy Spacek version. All the party stores sell fake blood that's made mostly with food dye and corn syrup. Amy bought a bottle for me and I poured it over my head and let it drip down a dress I hate. It looked creepy, and I got a lot of compliments, but the truth is I didn't feel like going to the parties. Five months ago you couldn't have kept me from going out, now I can barely muster the energy. I went because I saw it as an escape and a chance to be semi-normal for a few hours.

Amy and I slept in Gio's quad and he and Nat took us to lunch at this burger place where you create your own burgers or mac and cheese. Total pig-out village, but the food was great, and again, I felt normal for a few hours.

I know another big fight is coming because I want to visit Theresa. She was the shrink who stepped in front of a bullet for me. She's home from rehab now, and she's still recovering. I heard my father tell my mother that Theresa has physical and occupational therapists come to her house every day for a couple of hours each. I don't know how much time she spent in the hospital, or that in-treatment rehab center, but it had to be weeks in the hospital and months in rehab. Anyway, I don't care what my parents say. I'm going to visit her if I have to shout the house down.

They can't understand that the weight of gratitude and guilt crushes me. I'll never be able to repay what Theresa did. And though he'd never tell me if I asked, and I don't bother to ask since he never tells me, I know my father paid for and pays for her care. Which means she's getting the best. But even if everything returns to normal physically, how do you recover from a trauma like that? No doubt, she'd going to need to go to a shrink for a long time.

Next week I start with my new therapist, and I'm not looking forward to it. Between what happened with Theresa, and being yanked away from Chiara, who I really liked, I don't want to start that process again with anyone else. Not that I don't need it. I do. I know I'm fucked up. Who wouldn't be after the past few months, but the whole opening up to a stranger you have to trust to make the therapy meaningful doesn't appeal anymore. I know I have to try, but right now I can't work up the energy to care.

Before my mom or nonna comes knocking, I'm going to say good night and ask a question. When I said I'd give anything to have the freedom you enjoy, why did you shut down?

Buona notte.

Miffy

Six Day Earlier
Di Caro Residence
Dutchford
Sofia

Sofia knew she should be happy for her brother Gio and his new fiancée, Natalia, or as the family had taken to calling her, Nat. Well, *Nonna* and Dad called her Natalia, but that was because both of them had Dark Ages mentality, which was the root cause of Sofia's misery. She knew she was being mean when she cringed inside every time someone at this monster-sized party made a toast to the happy couple, but she couldn't help it. She liked Nat, she really did. Aside from being a blonde bombshell – well, half blonde, the red was growing out – Nat was smart as fuck and attended Brown University with Gio, who mooned after her. But right now was not the time to rub love in Sofia's face. She'd been back home for three weeks after being ripped away from the one person who saw her for who she really was, and had fallen for her.

Oh shit. Here comes Nonna. Gio called their grandmother the little general, and he wasn't kidding. Barely five feet tall and built like a mini linebacker, *Nonna* did not play. She could be funny and loving, but no one got cut any slack.

"*Cara.*" This was going to be bad. When *Nonna* spoke in Italian, even though her English was perfect, it meant she was dead serious as opposed to her usual absolutely serious. In Italian: "Stop moping around. You're wearing a pretty dress. Your hair is shiny, and you're a beautiful girl. Start acting like it."

Sofia stopped herself from rolling her eyes, smiled at her grandmother then said, "Okay, *Nonna*," when she wanted to say, "How I look is irrelevant. I feel like shit, and you know why." But Sofia would never say that or anything approximating that to anyone except Gio. And, maybe, Nat. Definitely not Aurora, the "little" sister who was more gansta than a high school sophomore at Our Lady Catholic High School For Girls. Ro never cut anyone slack either.

Thank God the seniors' classes were held on the third floor of the school, and they ate lunch later than the underclass girls. Sofia saw Ro when they travelled to and from school, and that was it. Bad enough they had to sit in the backseat of a blacked-out SUV driven by one of their father's thugs. That humiliation took a half hour to wear off each morning. Right about when homeroom ended. To have Ro know what Sofia was thinking and feeling would be an invitation to an emotional disaster from which she would never recover. Ro would never be Sofia's confidante.

The middle child, Sofia had always been the good girl. Polite. Quiet. An "A" student. *Delicate*. She hated that word. It intimated she didn't have the guts to stand up to life. That she had to be protected and cossetted as if she were a porcelain vase wobbling precariously on a broken stand. She'd had no control over the genetics that made her look as she did. She favored her mother's side of the family where the women were short in stature, small-boned, and fair skinned. No lie, Sofia was more than a foot shorter than her brother, who towered over her at six-four. If it weren't for her features, which were all Mom's except for the blue eyes, and even they weren't as bright as her father's and Gio's, Sofia didn't look like she belonged in the family photos.

No *poor me* shit here. Facts layered with living with a grandmother and father who wouldn't mind putting a chastity belt on her until she was twenty-five and married to a guy they chose.

Nat walked over and leaned against the wall next to Sofia and motioned to the packed house. "I'm told this isn't the full complement. That a bunch of folks couldn't make it on such short notice."

Sofia had to smile. Nat was trying to cheer her up. See. Good person. "Most of us live within a hundred-mile radius of here, but some are in Sicily, England, Canada, and California. They need more than three weeks to get their shit together to show up."

"Still, there has to be nearly three hundred people here. It's nice of them to come."

Now Sofia laughed. "Free food and booze, fancy digs, an excuse to dress up and show off, and a chance to see who the heir to the throne is marrying." Nat dipped her head and chuckled. "You think my father doesn't notice who doesn't make it?" Nat raised her brows. She had such an expressive face. "*No one* wants to be on his shit list."

"Ah."

"Exactly. Ah."

"Listen, Gio and I were wondering if you wanted to hang with us on Halloween. There are a few parties we're going to, and everyone is dressing up. You can bunk in Gio's room. Howie volunteered to crash on the couch, which is par for the course, so don't feel like you're putting him out of his space."

"If, and this is a giant if, I'm allowed to go –"

"Gio already talked to your parents. They're fine with it."

"What did he have to promise? Tommie the goon has to be there? I have to be handcuffed to my brother all night?"

Nat cracked up. "I'm sorry. I'm not laughing at you, really. This is me adjusting to the different levels of drama."

"Advice. Nothing happens in this family that doesn't have drama attached to it, including changing the brand of toilet paper we use." Sofia huffed. "You should have been here when Ro announced the toilet paper fell apart too easily. After ten minutes of her arguing with *Nonna*, Gio was so fed up he went to the Stop and Shop, bought six different brands of toilet paper, put them on the kitchen counter, told us to 'get a grip,' then disappeared. No lie, we spent an entire night fighting about the pros and cons of various toilet paper brands before picking one."

"Was your father involved in the toilet paper decision?"

"You're joking, right?" Nat shook her head. "He comes into the kitchen two minutes before dinner is on the table. He sits down, eats, gets up and poof. He's gone. Anything and everything that happens in or about the house is decided by Mom and *Nonna*."

"No conversation?"

Sofia almost smiled. Nat hadn't fully realized yet that while Gio looked exactly like their father, no one on earth could be more different. "Sometimes he asks about school. Most of the time, if he talks, it's to order us to do something Mom or *Nonna* wants us to do. Otherwise, he eats, kisses Mom on the cheek, and heads to who knows where."

Gio came over, leaned against the wall, and put his arm over Nat's shoulder. He was so gone for her. She was it for him, and Sofia had never seen her brother so happy.

"Yo, Soph, you coming with us on Halloween?"

Ah, an orchestrated approach. First send Nat to butter up Sofia, then Gio comes in for the close. "First you have to tell me how you convinced them to say yes. Especially since I'm missing school the next day."

"No convincing."

"Bullshit. Who's coming with me?"

"Amy, if you want."

In that moment, Sofia saw an opportunity she never thought would be possible. "Cool. I'll ask her."

The next morning, over breakfast, Sofia asked Gio and Nat to tell the story of how they met. She'd heard pieces of it about fifty times the night before, but she wanted to make sure she got the whole thing straight from the horses' mouths.

Lunchroom
Our Lady
Dutchford
Sofia

"I'm just sayin'." Amy stared at Sofia as if she wasn't processing. "If your father finds out, next time he's going to send you to an outpost in the Arctic. You sure you want to do this, Soph?"

"I have to for my sanity."

Amy took a deep breath and said, "Okay. Let's go over this slowly. I'm not as smart as you."

Sofia grinned. "You're slick and clever. I'm not worried about you keeping up." Amy made the get-on-with-it motion so Sofia broke it down. "Okay, here's how it works. You join The Letter Club and they assign a number *to you*. I'll write to Matteo using that number, give you the letters to mail, and he'll write return letters to you that you'll give to me."

"This is so fucking complicated. Why don't you get a burner phone and call him when you're in school?"

Sofia leaned on her elbow and laid her hand over her forehead. "When would you like me to buy the burner? When I'm shopping with my mom, or *Nonna*? If I'm shopping with you, Tommie's following us, so that's not happening. Even if I could get a burner, where should I keep it? The house is out, and I'm not allowed to drive anymore so I can't hide it in the car."

"I'll buy the burner for you."

"You'd have to keep it with you all week. Where do you propose to put it, and don't be rude." Amy rolled her eyes. "Our backpacks are searched coming in and at random during the day. The school's security guards go into our lockers whenever they want. You know the rules. No phones at school. You get busted you'll be suspended for three days. You want to explain that to your mother knowing how understanding and supportive Monica is?" Sofia glared at Amy.

"Oh, all right. I'm going to have to scope the mail before my 'rents, but that's doable." Amy twirled her long auburn hair around her finger. "Hey, how are you going to let him know what he has to do on his end?"

"Halloweenie."

"Huh?"

"When we're in Providence with Gio and Nat –"

"You should call them one name. NatGio, like National Geographic."

"Ooo." Sofia smacked Amy's arm. "That's a good one. Ro's gonna be pissed she didn't think of it."

Amy licked her forefinger and made a slash in the air. "Soph, one. Brat, zippo."

Sofia laughed. She absolutely loved Amy. "Yeah, for today anyway. But, for real, when we're in Providence, I'll call Matteo on your phone and tell him the whole plan. Don't worry, I'll give you the money to cover the call."

"I'm not worried. I'll hound your skinny ass until you do."

"Speaking of asses, you should've seen Nat in that dress Saturday. Holy fucking shit. Kim and J Lo have nothing on my future sister-in-law."

"I thought you said she has a rack."

"She does."

"Your brother is in heaven."

"For sure. He practically pants when he's next to her."

Amy laughed loud then said, "I'd love to find a guy who pants over me."

I'm working on nailing mine down.

Eight more months and Sofia would be her own woman. She'd be eighteen and done with high school. She couldn't wait to get the fuck out of Dutchford and as far away from the Dark Ages as possible.

The bell rang and they had to get to class. Sofia squeezed Amy's hand, and they went in opposite directions.

On the way home, Sofia told Ro about NatGio.

"Amy came up with it, right? You don't think like that."

"Whatever. It's perfect though."

"Only when you're referencing them as a couple. You can't call them that to their face, especially when the other one isn't there. It wouldn't make sense. It's cool, but it has limited applications."

Sofia should've known better than to try to talk to her sister as if she were a normal person.

The next day, Amy reported that she'd read The Letter Club's FAQs on their webpage, and she'd signed up online. By tonight they'd email her number, which meant Sofia had a number. She could hardly wait until Thursday afternoon. Only two and a half days until she'd be able to talk to Matteo, who, on that perfect night when they'd walked and talked for eight hours, had pushed up her sleeve and had written his phone number on the inside of her upper arm. She'd copied the number onto the inner cups of three bras and the backs of two pair of underpants figuring her father wouldn't go through her *personals*.

Her father. When he looked at her he saw a fragile victim. He had no idea who his middle child was at heart, and she had no intention of sharing that information with him. Even if she were so inclined, it wouldn't matter anyway. He'd made up his mind about her, and once Don Alessandro decided something, that was that.

What to wear for Halloween wasn't so much a decision as a chore. She hated the store-bought costumes, so she had to create something from out of her closet. She started in the back where she put all the dresses her mother and *Nonna* had bought. All fem and flowy. Shit Sofia would never buy for herself. She came upon a pink (blech) sheath with spaghetti straps that reminded her of the dress in the original *Carrie*. Another thing almost nobody knew about Sofia: she loved horror movies.

The more she thought about it, the more the idea appealed. She'd ask Amy to buy the fake blood, and she'd pour it over her head and let it drip down the dress. She wasn't blonde like Sissy Spacek, but Sofia's hair was a light enough brown that she could pull this off.

The next day in the cafeteria, she told Amy, "Don't forget to stop at the florist and get a wrist corsage."

Amy looked at Sofia like she'd lost her mind. "Are you feeling all right?"

"Sure. Why?

"You seem way too happy about pouring blood over your head and fucking up a new dress."

"It's colored corn syrup, and the dress should have never found its way into my closet. Wait 'til you see the thing. Country club little miss. It's a disgusting excuse of a garment."

"What did they feed you in Sicily? It's like you're fierce about everything."

"My shrink told me to take back my power. So I'm all over that shit."

"I don't think pouring blood all over you is what she had in mind."

"My asshole ex wanted to shoot me and nearly killed my therapist. I have two choices, Ames. Either I hide in my bedroom for the rest of my life or I take control of my destiny."

"Wild guess here, but you're going for door number two."

"I'll tell you one thing about living in Sicily, I saw what allowing yourself to be controlled looked like at the beginning, middle, and end of your life, and I want no part of it. I know you didn't understand why I stayed with that piece of shit after he hit me, but it happened twice. The first time, the minute after he did it, he got down on his knees in front of me and cried his eyes out. I heard so many 'I'm-so-sorry, I'll-never-do-it-again-I-swear,' that I thought he meant it and I gave him another chance. The second time it happened I went to Gio. I was a mess, for sure. But it was more because I was humiliated that I believed that shitbag than getting hit. Now I know better. No matter what, from now on, I decide my fate."

"Eight months from now."

"Don't remind me. I feel like I'm living seven hundred years ago. No wonder my father took me to Sicily. They're frozen in time back there. They're worse than old-school in their thinking, they're fucking medieval."

"Not to get you more torqued than you already are, but won't you be getting that with Matteo?"

Sofia laughed. "God, no. He hasn't lived there for nearly ten years. He went to Eton and Cambridge. He speaks English with a British accent. He's back in Sicily because his two older brothers died in a boating accident and he feels obligated to help his father. He's not going to stay there forever. Maybe a year or two."

"And where will you be?"

"Ah, duh. In college."

"Soph, I love you. No question. But think straight. If he's there and you're in school somewhere in the States, how's that going to work? He's a man. According to you, a gorgeous one. He's not going to keep it in his pants for years. You okay with him banging randoms to keep him from getting blue balls?"

The bell rung before Sofia could answer. Good thing too, since she didn't really have an answer. She'd been so sure Matteo had fallen for her, none of what Amy had brought up had even crossed Sofia's mind.

Shit.

Parisi Family Home
Vittoria, Sicily
Matteo

Standing on the stone balcony of his second-story suite of rooms, Matteo took a deep breath of sea air and for at least the hundredth time replayed that night a little more than three weeks ago that changed his life. A couple of months ago, shortly after he returned to his father's house, he'd heard Don Alessandro's family was staying with relatives in Vittoria after their eldest daughter's ex-boyfriend had tried to kill her. Talk about bloody crazy. Going after Don Alessandro's daughter? Completely barking mad. Matteo had meant to go over and pay his respects to the family, but there had been more to do than he'd expected. His father was inconsolable after the loss of his two eldest sons, and Matteo's mother had been dead since he was eleven years old. He was the only one left to shoulder what his father couldn't bring himself to do. With more paperwork than should be allowed, Matteo was left to handle all the arrangements for his brothers' memorial service and everything else that went along with it. By the time he'd gotten the time to meet the Di Caro family, they had returned to the States, and only Sofia remained in Vittoria.

Their initial meeting was innocent enough. Enzo and Valentina Conti, and their teenage daughter, Mia, were all in attendance when Matteo approached the family after Sunday Mass. As the usual pleasantries were exchanged, he overheard Sofia and Mia saying they were going to the beach on Tuesday after school. While he thought Sofia was pretty, she was too young and too delicate. Not his type, and the timing couldn't have been worse.

Serendipity, fate, God's hand…Matteo didn't know what force orchestrated what happened two days later on a Tuesday afternoon, but looking back, it seemed inevitable, even though so many decisions had been last minute.

He'd been in town all day taking care of mundane bullshit, when he'd gotten a hankering for pastries and coffee. He'd turned onto *Via Ruggero Settimo* to go to his favorite *pasticceria* before he had to visit one of the family's attorneys when he'd heard what he thought was Sofia's voice. He turned his head and saw her coming out of an upscale women's clothing store with Mia – obviously they didn't go to the beach. Two men were walking behind them, and Matteo had no doubt they were guarding Sofia at Don Alessandro's behest. Matteo didn't have the time or the inclination to approach the young women, and he ducked into the *pasticceria* without acknowledging them. After he placed his order, he went to the back of the shop to use the WC, and when he came out, he bumped into Sofia in the narrow hallway.

"Pardon," he muttered, cursing under his breath that of all the people he'd almost mowed down, it had to be her.

"Wow. You speak English."

"Clearly."

"British English." She scrunched her nose like a thoughtful rabbit: quick and endearing.

Where the hell did that thought come from?

"Perceptive."

"Are you opposed to speaking in full sentences, or is there a disability I need to be aware of so I don't make fun of you and feel crap about it after I find out you're suffering from some rare disease."

He shook his head and sighed. *Why?*

Why was his heart tripping in his chest? Why was his stomach doing somersaults? Why the fuck now?

The thought of telling her, in detailed paragraphs, all the things he'd like to do to her hit his groin like an internal hammer and his knees almost buckled.

He couldn't, shouldn't, and wouldn't.

"Thank you for asking so tactfully. I am not suffering from a disability, and, as you can now discern, I am quite capable of speaking in complete sentences. Good day, Ms. Di Caro." He took a step toward her to walk past her.

"Good day?"

He stopped and cursed that she wasn't as pliant as she looked.

"Are you unfamiliar with the term? Would saying bye-bye be more within your lexicon?"

She let out a high, sharp laugh. "Holy shit. A full-fledged look-down-your-nose upper-crust British snob in Vittoria, Sicily. This is rich."

He should have let it go. He knew better. He really did. "I'm neither British nor a snob. I'm trying to be polite given our proximity in this small space, and I'm mindful that you must be in need of the loo, or else you wouldn't be here."

"The *loo*? I might pee in my pants from laughing so hard at your language usage, but I'm back here pretending I have to use the bathroom so I can escape Cro-Magnon man one and two for a few minutes."

"Is that wise?"

"What are the odds that my ex, who's in prison in Connecticut, would have escaped, fled the country, arrived in Sicily, made it to Vittoria, and happened to be hanging out in this back hallway in a tiny pastry shop waiting to try to shoot me again without me knowing it?"

What she'd told him boggled his mind. "I'll grant you, not particularly high. However –"

"Please. No lectures. No sound reasoning. No homilistic edification about the sanctity of my safety for my parents' peace of mind."

"I wouldn't dare."

She gave him a butter-wouldn't-melt smile.

"But I would like to point out that you are a young woman in a foreign country, and being alone is not particularly smart."

"Gee thanks. I love it when a man tells me I'm an idiot."

"I did not state or insinuate any such thing."

She straightened her spine and said in her version of a British accent, "I beg to differ."

He chuckled. "Touché."

"If you're so worried about my safety, come find me at midnight when I sneak out and walk the grounds near Enzo and Valentina's house." Exaggeratingly, she fluttered her eyelashes. "Good day, Matteo Parisi." She went into the loo and locked the door.

Matteo turned away to face the back of the hallway and rearranged himself. When he turned back, he strode out to the counter, asked to have his pastries placed in a bag. *Sacrilege.* He left the *pasticceria* and never looked to see if Mia or the Don's men were about. He should have. He should have told them what Sofia did at night. He should have called Enzo and informed him. He should have called his father and had him call Don Alessandro.

He should have been smart and circumspect and behaved as an adult.

Instead, like a randy teenager, he waited in the dark until he saw her walking along the edge of the property. He went to great lengths to make himself known without frightening her. When he stepped out of the shadows, she stated, "It took you bloody long enough."

As he reexamined every misstep that took him to her that night, his phone rang. The number was international and from the States. He had a few mates who'd moved to New York who knew his habit of staying up until all hours, so he answered the call.

"You're standing on the balcony, aren't you?"

"Miffy."

"You're still not sleeping, are you?"

"Where are you?"

"In Providence with my brother, his fiancée, and Amy."

"Your brother is engaged?"

"Long story, and I don't have much time."

"I don't like breaking promises."

"You made your promise to my father under duress."

That was a lie, the truth of which he could never share with her. "Nonetheless."

"Write this down."

He walked back into his rooms, found a pen, and pulled out a pad. "What am I writing?"

"Go to The Letter Club's website. Sign up. Get a correspondent's number then text your number to this phone." Then she gave him the phone number. "I'll write to you through TLC and it will be anonymous. No one can trace the letters. TLC acts like a clearinghouse. We'll talk without talking. You'll be keeping your promise."

"I promised no contact."

"Is that what you want?"

He heard the longing in her voice and it tugged at him right down to his marrow. "It's what is necessary."

"Because *he* said so?"

"No. Because it's the right thing to do." Silence. Shit. "Do you trust me?"

"What does that have to do with this?" She sounded near tears. Oh hell.

"You have to trust that your safety and happiness are paramount to me. Honouring that is everything."

"Then do this for me. It'll make me happy and it's safe. Look at the FAQ page. We use numbers instead of names. We address the letters to TLC and they send them on. No return addresses, no tracking down the senders."

"Sofia."

"Matt. Please."

He closed his eyes and wished for things that could never be. For him to be free of his obligations. More importantly, for them not to exist because his brothers were alive. To be back in London, living his life. For her to be old enough, which would mean her father wouldn't want to kill him for feeling as he did.

Since wishing did not make it so, he sighed, knowing he would give her this. He'd write to her every now and again as she moved on with her life and he became a memory. *But she will always be his.* In the broken heart he carried in his aching chest, she would always be the shining light that could mend all the cracks in his soul. He knew she was better off without him, and he'd ease her into that. He'd used the letters to guide her away from him.

"All right." He heard her sob and wanted to curse, break something, get on a plane, cross the Atlantic, scoop her up, and disappear. Instead, he made it worse for both of them. "Hold my hand, little rabbit. I won't let go."

Halloween Party
Somewhere in Providence
Sofia

"Thank God." Amy grabbed Sofia's hand and dragged her into a corner of the kitchen where the music wasn't blaring. "I was having a hell of a time trying to explain to Nat what she thought she heard through the bathroom door."

"What did she think she heard?"

"You sobbing."

Well, fuck. "Guilty. Hearing his voice, asking him to do this…so hard." She fought back the tears as she clutched Amy's phone to her chest. "Too hard."

"The good news is you have blood running down your face so your red eyes don't really show. The bad news, I'm sure Nat didn't believe me when I told her it was probably toilet noise she heard. Be prepared. Your brother is going to find you and quiz you."

"Here." Sofia pressed Amy's phone into her hand. "Thanks."

"Did he say he'd do it?"

She nodded even though she wasn't positive he'd go through with it. "I told him to text his assigned correspondent's number to your phone."

Amy grabbed Sofia's hand and tugged. "Let's go back to the party. So far you've been a hit."

Sofia motioned up and down at Amy's body. "You're the one catching all sorts of attention. Maybe you'll find that guy to pant over you."

"Please. Who doesn't have a 'play doctor' fantasy?"

"Ames. You're in a flesh-colored body suit, a lab coat that's wide open and hits mid-thigh, and you're wearing bright red stilettos. You have a stethoscope tied in a knot around your neck and lipstick that matches your shoes. I'm thinking this is a 'play doctor' fantasy at a BDSM club."

Amy laughed, and as they moved through the crowd, Sofia was having an out-of-body experience. She knew she was in some student dive house, probably a bunch of guys given the state of the kitchen and…yuck, bathroom. Yet, in her heart and mind, she was standing on that balcony with Matteo. Actually, she wished they were in his flat in London living the life he'd left behind. The way he'd described it, she knew he yearned to return to the city he called home. Three weeks and two days had passed she'd been with him, but she remembered their never-ending conversation as if everything that happened had been only three hours ago.

When he'd stepped out from behind the hedge, her stomach had done Olympic diving flips. She didn't think he would come, but she'd hoped. When he smiled, she thought someone had turned on all the floodlights. She'd never tell him she'd been thinking up ways to get Valentina to invite him to dinner. The moment Sofia laid eyes on him outside of church, she wanted him. In a split second she knew all those dates she'd gone on, the boyfriends, the sneaking around, Walter, before he lost his mind, was all child's play. Matteo Parisi was the real deal from head to toe.

Good looks had never impressed her. Blessed with an abundance of TDH relatives, most of whom would be favorites to win the Gorgeous Alpha of the Year award, she knew along with those swoony hot looks came arrogance and a level of stupidity when it came to women that was hard to believe twenty years into the new millennium.

Matteo seemed different. True, he had classic Mediterranean looks, soulful caramel-tinted brown eyes, a little bit more than scruff, but not quite a beard, and lips women paid a shit ton of money to have. But unlike the archetype, he gave off a cool, laid-back, don't-worry-be-happy vibe. Which made those proper British manners and posh accent that much more striking.

"Where to?" he asked.

He shook his head as she pushed her way past him through the hedge, then pointed to the curvy hillside lane. "Up." They walked for a few minutes in silence before she asked, "How long you visiting for?"

He drew in a deep breath as if she'd asked him to break down the Theory of Relativity. "I'm not visiting. I'm here for a while."

She tilted her head and he chuckled. "What's so funny?"

"You scrunch up your nose like a twitchy rabbit."

"Earlier I wasn't 'particularly smart' and now I'm a 'twitchy rabbit.' I don't know if I can handle this much flattery."

He stopped and put his hands on hips his jeans hugged like a lover. "It's endearing." She fluttered her lashes as if she were a silly girl. "You don't like criticism and you don't take compliments well. Our conversation will be somewhat limited, I fear."

"Don't be afraid. Let it rip. I'm well practiced at verbal warfare."

"I have no doubt." He resumed walking and she fell in beside him.

"So. Why are you here for a while?"

"Family...matters."

"What's with the word choice delay? I told you, let it rip."

"Some things are private."

"Oh." Now she felt bad. "Sorry."

They walked up the incline, and she veered off to the left.

"Where are you going, Miffy?"

She stopped at the edge of the road and stared at him. "You're stealth. You sneak 'em in, don't you? Is that the droll British humor I've heard about?"

His lips twitched. "Something like that."

"If I remember my picture books correctly, Miffy is the little rabbit who likes to draw."

"Well done you."

She stuck her chin out. "I like it. She has lots of good friends, and she loves visiting her grandparents. You could've chosen worse."

"I intended the moniker to be something to make you smile."

She did. She smiled.

"There you go. Quite lovely."

"I have to ask. Do you ever curse?"

He laughed. "Frequently."

"I mean more than bloody or sod off. That's right, isn't it? Sod off."

"It is, and I do. I have a full arsenal in British English, American English, Italian, and Sicilian dialect. Take your pick."

She walked over to the four boulders that someone had to've moved together to make a perfect seating with a great view of the city, the beach, and the sea. "Give me the worst in British English."

"Tosser, wanker, slag, chav, minger."

"Don't know any of them, but they don't sound too awful."

"Trust me. In context, at least three, if not four of them would start a fight."

"Do you say fuck and shit?"

"All the time, but the British insult can be subtle yet more insidious than the American curses. It's all about usage."

She climbed up on a boulder and motioned for him to do the same. *"How old were you when you moved there?"*

"My family didn't move there. I went to school there."

"Which school?"

"Eton College, then Cambridge."

"Two colleges?"

"Eton College is what you would call a prep school in the States."

"How old were you when you went to Eton?"

"Thirteen."

"Damn, that's young. Did you want to go?"

He shrugged. *"Not particularly, but my mother had died about eighteen months earlier and my father thought it would keep me out of trouble."*

"Soph." Someone was shaking her. "Soph. What the fuck?" Gio. Her brother was shaking her shoulder, forcing her to leave that glorious night. In that moment she hated him for bringing her back to the now.

She batted his hand and he dropped it from her shoulder. "I'm fine. Zoning. That's all. Can't a girl get a little head space?"

Gio's brows drew together. "It took me like a full minute to bring you back from wherever you were. You sure you're okay?"

"In relative terms, yeah. But overall? Not even close. Do I need to recap?"

He shook his head. "Nat said you were crying in the bathroom."

"I was coughing in the bathroom because this house needs to be dipped in bleach."

Gio gave her a lopsided smile. "Eight college dudes in a house is not a recipe for cleanliness."

"You think?"

He took her hand. "C'mon. We're movin' on."

They rounded up Amy and Natalia and climbed into Gio's new ride, a 2017 Lexus RC 300.

As Gio headed to the next party, Amy asked, "Being nosy, I know, but what happened to the Ferrari?"

Gio looked at Nat and lifted his chin. She answered. "I have a half scholarship and my money was running low. Gio sold the Ferrari to pay for the rest."

"Damn," Amy drew out the word. "That's huge love."

Gio lifted Nat's hand and put her fingers to his lips and glanced over at her. She dropped her chin and tilted her head toward him. More gooey, swoony shit Sofia didn't need to witness. Would she ever be rid of this torture?

At least the next party was at a hotel, and they had a good DJ. The dance floor was packed with people in fantastic costumes. Amy grabbed Sofia's hand and yanked her into the throng of gyrating bodies. It took about two minutes and a couple of super handsome slick guys dressed in tuxes with tails joined them. It took Sofia a few beats to figure out why they looked familiar. Darius and Nathaniel, two of Gio's quad-mates. She wondered if her brother sent them. When she visually located Gio, who was taller than most of the people in the room, she saw he was wrapped around Nat, grinding on her. Those two were nauseating.

Sofia leaned over to Amy and told her who the guys were. Amy gave them a finger wave, to which Nathaniel winked. That was all it took, they broke away and were dancing together, drifting off into the crowd.

"You want something to drink?" Darius sort of yelled at Sofia.

She nodded, and they went into the hallway where the noise level lowered by ten decibels, and the bars were set up. "Hi, Darius."

He smiled. He had the whitest teeth she ever saw. "What are you drinking?'

"Ginger ale would be great."

He told the bartender their drink order, then passed her drink to her, took his beer and they walked until they found a bench where they could sit.

"You look elegant," she told him.

"You look scary as fuck," he replied.

She laughed. "I'm still feeling a bit gory."

"Understandable."

"So what's doing in your life?"

They wound up talking about his new girlfriend, who was studying stage and production management at Emerson College in Boston. He wasn't gushy, but Sofia couldn't help but think, yet another smack in the face. The entire world was hooking up and coupling off.

By the time they made it back to Gio's dorm, it was nearly two in the morning. Nat yawned then waved her hand in front of her face. "You guys want to shower? I've gotta wash this gunk off me."

She had green globby stuff all over the white sheet wrapped around her toga style. She was the ghost, and Gio was the ghostbuster. Sofia had watched him chase her around one of the houses, his giant water gun slung over his shoulder. Everyone laughed as Nat screeched as she ran up the stairs. That was the last thing they heard until a half hour later she and Gio came down the steps looking disheveled. They fucked so much Sofia didn't know how they were able to walk.

Nat stowed a big towel with gunk on it that she'd put over the passenger seat of the car, and walked into her and Gio's "annex" room, which was really her dorm room. Someone, probably Howie, had cut a door-size hole in the wall, and hung a door with an industrial-strength lock. The quad's "annex" room was born, and Gio and Nat were living together on campus. Only Gio could pull off that kind of shit, make it look easy, and never get in trouble.

"Here," Nat called. "Come get clean towels."

After they'd showered and said their good nights, Amy and Sofia climbed into Howie and Gio's beds. Howie, who was watching a *Chopped* marathon, had waved from the quad's sofa and that was the extent of their communication.

Amy muttered, "'Night, Soph," turned over, and two minutes later she was snoring lightly.

Sofia should have been exhausted. She'd been up since six in the morning, and had gone to school all day before coming down to Providence. But her brain wouldn't shut down. Hearing Matteo's voice on the phone had been exquisite torture. It took no time for her mind to go right back to where she'd been before her brother had pulled her out of her trance.

"Did you get into trouble a lot?"

Matteo shrugged. "I'd gotten a bit wild after my mother died. Mischief mostly, but my dad had his hands full and worried he couldn't give me the attention I needed. I hadn't been keen on going away, especially to England, but it didn't take long for me to feel glad I was there."

"Because?"

"I see a career in journalism in your future."

"I see a guy avoiding a question."

He shook his head. "Not avoiding, deflecting."

Shit. She felt bad again. "Is that private too?"

"A little. But I don't mind telling you." She pulled up her knees and wrapped her arms around them. "I'm the youngest. Ten years between my next oldest brother and me. My father spent most of his time with my brothers, who wanted nothing to do with me, a little kid. I was my mother's bambino. *When we lost her, I felt like I was on my own. When I went to Eton, I was surrounded by contemporaries, many of whom were far from their families, and I didn't feel alone anymore."*

Geez. Now she really felt bad. "Did you speak English before you went?"

"Enough. Between school, TV, and the movies, I understood the students and, for the most part, they understood me. I had the most trouble understanding the Scots."

She nodded. "We had an exchange student in our school from Glasgow a couple of years ago. I got about every tenth word."

He chuckled and the sound made her want to tell jokes all night. She liked being the one making him happy.

That thought and the expression on his gorgeous face when he laughed gave her enough peace to close her eyes and drift off to sleep.

Gio's Quad
Brown University
Sofia

Sofia was surprised when she got up and saw the connecting door to
Gio and Nat's room ajar. She knocked, walked in, saw the made bed
and gave herself a mental slap. They had gone to class. Somewhere
in the back of her brain she remembered Gio saying they'd have
lunch together. She walked into the quad's main room and looked up
at the giant clock above the couch. Shit. It was nearly noon. She ran
back to Howie's bed and shook Amy.

"You gotta get up. We're supposed to be ready for lunch in a half
hour."

"Go eat without me," Amy mumbled and pulled the covers over
her head.

"Get. Up." Sofia shoved Amy's shoulder. "After we eat, we're
going home."

"Jesus. All right." Amy swung her legs over the side of the bed.
"What time is it?"

"Noon."

"You have the room key?"

"Yeah. Grab your towel and stuff. We gotta go down the hall to
the bathroom and get ready."

Amy pulled her phone out from under the pillow and looked at
the screen.

"Anything?"

She shook her head.

Shit. If Matteo had done what Sofia had asked right away, he
should have his correspondent's number by now. All she could do
was wait. And hope.

Forty minutes later, as Sofia and Amy were making the beds,
Gio and Nat came into the quad.

"I can't believe you had the energy to get up so early to go to
class," Sofia told them.

Nat dropped her backpack on the sofa and plopped down next to it. "We barely dragged our asses out of here, and I can't speak for your brother, but concentrating and focusing was spotty."

Gio yawned then said, "Yeah. I need fuel. C'mon. We're going to Luxe Burger." They left the dorm, walked forever to the car, piled in, and headed into town.

Sofia never saw burgers like this. You could build your own, and waiters were carrying plates with burgers that were six inches high. Gio said he was too tired to figure out which ingredients he wanted on his burger, so he ordered the M.O.A.B., the Mother Of All Burgers, with a side of cheddar tater tots. They also had build your own mac and cheese, which was what the girls did.

Apparently, Gio had called home that morning and arranged for Sofia and Amy to be picked up at the restaurant at three. Even early in the morning, he had been starving and knew he wanted to eat at Luxe Burger. The guy had Nat and food – in that order – on the brain 24/7. How he had room to cram in studying and lacrosse practice amazed Sofia.

Exactly at three, Tommie, one of her father's "men," pulled up in a blacked-out SUV. She hated those damn things and everything they stood for. She hugged Gio and Nat as they said their good-byes, turned and let Amy precede Sofia into the car. They sat in the middle row and off they went. Back home. Or prison, as Sofia had taken to calling it in her mind.

God bless Amy. Between a mac and cheese food coma, and her being deprived of her beauty sleep, she went out within five minutes of them being on the road. Which left Sofia the quiet she needed to return to that night and Matteo.

They sat on the rocks for a while. He pointed out places in the city and asked her about home.

"We live in Connecticut near the Massachusetts border. It's a boring little place with all the usual stuff you see in the suburbs. It's pretty and gets real green in the spring and summer, and in the fall, it's gorgeous. If you're into horseback riding, it's a great place to live. Lots of ranches and stables. I like the city better. It takes about an hour to get to Boston, depending on traffic. That's where I want to go to college."

"Harvard?"

"Actually, Tufts. They have the School of the Museum of Fine Arts."

He leaned back and regarded her intently. "You're an artist?"

She shrugged. "I draw and transfer my work to woodcuts to make prints. I'm an Albrecht Dürer fan. Since I've been here in Sicily, I've drawn a lot, but I haven't been able to do any woodcuts or print work. I miss it."

"I can remedy that. Tell me what you need, and I'll have it sent to your Zio's house."

"My Zio's house is part of the problem. There's no place I can set up my studio and not be disturbed. I'm a prisoner there."

"That's not true. You were in the city today shopping."

"And Cro-Magnon men one and two are always with me. Before the shooting, I had some freedom. My father's crazy about security, but at least I had a life and a studio where no one bothered me. Now." She shook her head. "I have to resort to sneaking out to sit up here to get some alone time."

"Unfortunately, my little rabbit, the world is a dangerous place. You better than most know how violent it can be. You cannot fault your father for wanting to protect you from the harm I'm sure he feels he should have been able to keep from invading your life in the first place."

"I don't 'fault' him for wanting to keep me safe. I 'fault' him for suffocating me to the point where I'm ceasing to exist."

"Sofia."

"Okay. A little melodramatic, but I'd give anything to have the freedom you enjoy."

The look that crossed his face literally shuttered his expression and he became as still as the stones they were sitting on.

A horn honking behind the SUV pulled Sofia back into the car. She turned her head to see an arm waving out the window of a mom-mobile sitting at a stop sign. The car behind her must have been the honker. When Sofia turned to face forward, she saw they were close to Amy's house.

She shook Amy's arm. "Ame. Wake up. We're home."

"Already?" she mumbled.

"It's been an hour since we left Providence."

"Shit. I zonked, huh?"

"Ah, yeah." Sofia put her hand next to Amy's knee and pointed to her backpack. Amy got the hint, opened it up, and checked her phone. "Anything?" Sofia mouthed. Amy nodded, fished around the bottom of her backpack, found a pen, lifted Sofia's jeans above her ankle, and wrote on her leg.

Tommie pulled up the driveway to Amy's house and Sofia gave her friend a giant hug and whispered in her ear, "Thank you for this. You're the best, Ames."

Amy squeezed back, shouldered her backpack, opened the door, and said, "Thank you, Tommie. I'll see you on Monday, Soph." She hopped out of the SUV and slammed the door.

As Sofia had done a hundred times since that night, she wondered what had prompted Matteo to shut down like that. He'd withdrawn completely for all of one minute. Then, like nothing had happened, he flipped a switch somewhere in his head and all the lights came back on.

It would be one of the things she'd ask him in her first letter.

Parisi Family Home
Vittoria, Sicily
Matteo

Miffy. It took eleven days for your letter to get here, and while I'd prefer the immediacy of a phone call or a Skype, I must say, receiving a handwritten letter certainly has an intimacy I didn't expect. I decided to hand-write mine to keep it mutual.

All Hallows Eve, and Samhain started in the UK, and it's observed, but not with the gusto you Yanks seem to have. There's a much bigger do about Guy Fawkes Day, or some call it Bonfire Night. Celebrations include parades, bonfires, and fireworks on November 5th. Many people get painted up and go out in costumes of the era, 1605, which was when the unveiling of a plot to blow up King James I and Parliament was uncovered. There's a lot of burning Guy Fawkes, one of the conspirators, in effigy.

From what I remember from when I was a small boy in Sicily, we celebrated All Souls Day on November 2nd in remembrance of our departed family members. Supposedly, the dead rise from their graves during the night between November 1st and 2nd to go back to their homes where they leave sweets and toys hidden inside the house for the children. Kids run around looking for the gifts the dead left for them like a treasure hunt.

Simpler times when we were truly free. You can have mobility and all the communication devices in the world at your fingertips, but when you are burdened, freedom is relative. You asked why I shut down, and that is the answer. The burdens that brought me back weigh heavy. Something I know you understand well, and for that I am more sorry than I ever could express. I wish you never had to learn what it feels like to carry that kind of anguish. It's why I want you to try, really try, with the new therapist. Any relief you can achieve that lightens your soul has to be good. You are mere months away from hearing if you got into the college of your choice where you can explore your talents and expand your horizons. Learn. Find new mates who share common visions for the future. You have the power to set yourself free.

Promise me you will try and that you will give this new therapist a chance to help you.

I agree you should shout the house down for the right to see Theresa. That too will be therapy. You will be able to see she's whole and improving. You didn't do that to her, Miffy, a crazy person did. And before you say the crazy person wouldn't have been there but for you, remember, crazy doesn't need an excuse. They take the mundane and make it into something it is not.

Since time melts away when you are deep in your art, spend as many hours as you can in your studio. Study there too. Being surrounded by the implements of your craft will quiet your mind and make everything come easier.

You have it in you to soar.

So try.

Me

Di Caro Residence
The Studio
Sofia

Your letter took twelve days to get here, and I figure that a little less than two weeks is the turnaround time we should expect. Better than the Pony Express. Barely.

Tomorrow is Thanksgiving and we are going to have almost forty people here. Before I get into that noisy mess, I'll tell you some good news. I saw Theresa. And she looks wonderful.

Okay, let me back up. I knew if I asked my mom if I could go, she'd ask my dad. That's the way things work here. Talk about old school, and not in a good way. Anyway, since I figured he was the one who was going to make the decision, I sucked it up, and while we were eating dinner, I told him I wanted to see Theresa.

He's not a big talker to begin with, and he doesn't say much at dinner, which is supposed to be all happy-happy. I don't give a shit if it rocks his boat or gives him indigestion. If he's in charge, then I get to ask when he's available since who the fuck knows where he goes and what he does. When he's in his study, that's a no-fly zone, so dinner is the only time I have to hit him up.

I nearly fell out of my chair when he said he thought it was a good idea. Of course, I had to be driven over there, but the only limit on my visit was how long Theresa had the energy to see me.

If you saw her, you wouldn't believe she was shot. Of course, I didn't see what her chest looks like, but she was moving around like nothing happened. She said the physical therapists had been wonderful, and she's still seeing a PT now. The occupational therapy is new, but she doesn't think it will last long since her range of motion is good and she's able to cook for herself and take care of all her needs.

She lives alone, which worries me, but I didn't say anything. I saw an alarm code pad in the front hallway, so I know she has a security system. I didn't ask, but I bet my father took care of that too.

We talked about what happened and I lost it, which made me feel horrible, but she said I had to talk about it as much as I could until it didn't stop me from leading me life. Chiara had said the same thing, and so did you. So, yeah, I gave the new shrink a try.

Theresa knows her and says she'll help me. I went to her – her name is Sarah – once already and I go next week because she's gone for the Thanksgiving weekend. She's nice, but older than Theresa and Chiara. Like old enough to be their mother. I guess I should look at it as she has more experience, but it's going to take me a while to loosen up around her. But I promise, I'll try.

Theresa and I are going to have dinner at a restaurant together next week. Another small slice of normal, and since my father doesn't object to me seeing her, I got no pushback when I announced it to him over dinner. I swear, when I started talking, I saw his lips twitch. I had no idea I amused him, but since it seems to be going okay, I'm going to keep talking to him at dinner.

I never told you this: before he left Sicily to go home, he took me to lunch. Just me and him, which blew me away. He had never done that before. He was good company, and he was funny. Gio says Dad used to be looser when we were little, and that he was having a hard time with us growing up. The shooting changed everything. I know we can't rewind the clock, but I need normal so bad I want to scream.

Okay. Get ready.

Thanksgiving. When we have a battalion descend on us like rabid locusts. It's one of the few times Nonna doesn't cook. Not that she doesn't want to, she does, big time. She doesn't trust anyone else's cooking. She thinks some restaurants are okay, but even then, she has a running commentary about everything from the starch in the napkins to the dessert dishes. She doesn't cook for big family things because my father won't let her. All the food is catered. By the same place. Every. Time. Talk about trust issues, my father... Well, you know.

Since my mother's brothers and sisters and their families were here for Easter, my father's six sisters and their families are coming for Thanksgiving. All of them are married, and all of them had two kids, except for my Aunt Toni (Antonia). She has eight kids. EIGHT. KIDS. And not because she's so Catholic it hurts, but because my Aunt Toni, who I love with my whole heart, went earth mother hippie-dippy on the family and married an Israeli guy who grew up on a Kibbutz before he came to the States (where his parents were from) to go to college. That's where he met Toni.

I'm soooo sorry I wasn't alive and cogitating to have heard what had to have been about two years worth of screaming, yelling, shouting, and cursing – all from my dad. He's the oldest, and older than Toni by thirteen years. Their father died when Toni, the youngest, was seven or eight. My father's mother died before Aurora was born. That was sixteen years ago, and she's named for that nonna. *But, no doubt, my father became the head of that household when his dad died and my father was around twenty.*

Fast forward to when Toni brought Aaron home. This story Toni told me, and I laughed so hard I couldn't breathe.

Aaron was in law school, and Toni was a junior in college when she got pregnant. They had met halfway through her freshman year, and that was it. They were together for life.

To keep my father from killing Aaron, they went to Maryland and got married. It's one of the quickie states. You have to wait only two days between getting the license and getting hitched.

They got the license on a Friday and a hippie rabbi married them on Sunday. Toni said the only thing that kept my father from kicking an embolism was how happy their mother was that Toni was married. Apparently, my other nonna *was a sweet, easy-going woman. I'm sorry she isn't around now. We need sweet and easygoing here in a big way. She was a little upset they didn't get married in the Catholic church, but she liked Aaron, who was halfway to being a lawyer.*

Toni popped out that first kid when she was twenty. Then she waited until after she graduated college and Aaron had started working as an attorney before she lined up the rest of their brood. My cousin Adam, the oldest, is five years older than his sister, Ahava (yes, all of their first names begin with A). Three girls, five boys, in order: Adam, Ahava, Abraham, Akiva, Ariel, Asher, Adinah, and Alexander. I know. Why they gave up on the Hebrew names with Alex is a mystery.

Anyway, out of all my relatives, this group is my favorite. Gio and Ro's favorites too. They're the most normal, well-adjusted people you'll ever meet. They live in a big old farmhouse in New York a little more than an hour north of the city. They have only one car. For years it used to be an old Volvo station wagon. but recently, they bought a new electric SUV to make their carbon footprint as small as they can.

Aaron takes the train into the city every day to work and plays chauffeur on the weekends. They grow their own vegetables, are vegetarians, and they make Elizabeth Warren look conservative.

Adam is taking his PhD in math at MIT and he's coming with his fiancée, Leah, who is taking her PhD in brain and cognitive sciences at MIT. Yeah, complete brainiacs.

Adam's a couple of years older than Gio, and they're friends. I've heard Nat and Leah are like besties. If they weren't my relatives, I'd be intimidated being around all that brainpower. For real though, all Toni's and Aaron's kids are so cool.

We'll be in New York next month because Akiva is being bar mitzvahed. That's right. Toni's raising the kids Jewish. She told me it was important to Aaron and she didn't give a shit either way (her words).

I love watching the look on my father's face when that brood arrives. I swear, he still hasn't forgiven Aaron for knocking up Toni twenty-two years ago. It doesn't matter they're happy, have all those kids, and Aaron's this prominent civil rights lawyer. All my dad sees is Toni sitting in her mother's kitchen telling her mom and my father that she's married and pregnant.

You know what? I'm going to finish this after Thanksgiving. There's going to be some drama. There's always drama in our house. I'll let you know if we reach DefCon 1.

I'm back. And Thanksgiving did not disappoint. Dramarama.

The good news, Gio made sure we sat at the end of that enormous table with all of Toni and Aaron's kids, even Alex, who's five. He's the cutest kid. Big sandy blond curls his family calls his Jew-fro. He adores his sisters, who watch over him without hovering. I wish someone would've given my mother and Nonna those lessons.

The drama started when my aunt Bella (Isabella), who is the oldest girl and three years younger than my father, started in on her oldest son, Martin. Side note, Bella got married when she was in her mid-twenties. She met my uncle Ricky at work. She was a secretary at an insurance company, and he was a manager there. He's older than her by a lot. Like fifteen years. I don't know why he didn't get married sooner, but he was forty when they got hitched. Anyway, it *took my aunt like six years to get pregnant with Martin, and another three years before Andrew came along, so my cousins are twenty-two and nineteen. They live in Hartford – insurance capital of the world.*

It seems Martin, who got a job at the same insurance company his father works at, big surprise, is not an insurance superstar, and for whatever reason, Bella decided Thanksgiving at our house was a great place to embarrass the fuck out of Martin. One minute I heard Uncle Ricky saying – imagine how loud this had to be since we were at the other end of a huge table – "Let it go, Bella," and the next Martin jumps up, throws his napkin on the table, and shouts, "I hate that fucking job. I never wanted it in the first place. I liked managing the music store. There was no reason for me to give that up."

Aunt Bella: "What kind of a future would you have there? A lifetime of managing a little music store?"

Martin: "A fucking happy one." Then he marched out of the dining room and went to the backyard.

Bella got up to go after him. Uncle Ricky took her hand and told her, "Sit down, Bella. Let him be." To which Andrew – who hates being called Andy but is okay with Drew – says, "If only."

Nat tucked her lips in and looked at her plate to keep from laughing, Gio and Adam stared at each other, hollowing out their cheeks, Leah fiddled with her napkin, and Ro, Ahava (who's two months younger than me), and I made bug eyes at each other. My cousin Abe, who's fifteen and has hormone teenage boy brain, cracks up, which gets thirteen-year-old Akiva going, and Alex, who is too young to know what's happening but wants to keep up with his older brothers, starts giggling.

From the head of the table, my father shoots Aaron a glare that would melt an iceberg. As if Aaron, who's like fifteen chairs away from Abe, had anything to do with Abe's outburst. Like I said, Dad has never forgiven Aaron for enjoying Toni in college.

Aunt Bella starts to cry and runs from the table, and my father gives a minor head tilt, which is the signal for my mother to follow Bella and do damage control.

Eventually Bella returned to the table. When she did, Gio and Adam went outside to hang with Martin, and about a half hour later they all came back in, but Martin dragged his chair to our end of the table, and we returned to DefCon 4, because we are never at DefCon

5 in this house. That would mean everything is peaceful and normal. And we all know what bullshit that would be when it comes to my family.

Miffy

Parisi Family Home
Vittoria, Sicily
Matteo

This was why he fell in love with her. During that night, he had gotten a glimpse of all that spirit and humour waiting to breathe fresh air after she recovered from her ordeal, and more than anything, he wished he could be there when the doors opened to her soul. Selfishly, he wanted to be the one upon whom her light shone for eternity.

Sofia's letter made him laugh like he had fifteen-year-old "hormone teenage boy brain." He would have loved to have been there. Not so much to witness the drama, although it sounded rich, but to see her reaction and hold her hand while she made "bug eyes" at her cousins.

At a mitochondrial level, he ached over the impossibility of a "them." He could and would gladly wait for her to turn eighteen. Of all the reasons they couldn't be together, that was a matter of time measured and erased in mere months. But everything else – every other bloody fucking thing that would suck the lifeblood out of him by the time he finished doing what needed to be done – he would never put her in the position of being near that or him, and what he would become for having done it.

Now more than ever he would assume the mantle of being British. Stiff upper lip. No emotional outbursts. Suffer in silence. It went against everything he felt for her and wanted to do with her. But, for her, he would sacrifice everything so she could lead the life she deserved.

Which wouldn't include him.

Miff,
I have never laughed so hard at the written word. You are a gifted storyteller. I felt as if I was there, sitting next to you at the table. Don't forget to tell me how Akiva's bar mitzvah goes. I have had the pleasure of attending three, all relatives of mates from Eton.

Incredibly good news about Theresa. She sounds like a resilient woman. I have no doubt she will recover fully and return to her practice.

What's next for you? How many weeks until your winter break? I don't know the American school system, but I presume you have a couple of weeks to be with your family. And while that might make you crazy, it will provide colorful reading for me. Selfish, I know, but life is much quieter here than I'm used to.

My father eats dinner with me almost every evening, and that's the only time we see each other. He has slowly returned to work, and during the day he is busy with business, and I have my little companies to attend to. While I still have family and friends here, it isn't the same. It's been over nine years since I've lived here. Yes, I spent some winter holidays and summers here, but I worked in one of Father's factories during the summer, so there wasn't much time for socializing.

I'm grateful for modern technology. It makes it easy for me to visit with my mates, but again, it's not the same.

Recently, I've been spending my evenings rounding up street dogs and bringing them to a shelter run by a family a few miles out of town. They have the acreage to keep as many as one hundred dogs. Unlike Britain and the US, Sicily does not view dogs as part of the family. Many people abandon their dogs, and cats, when they are old, sick, or pregnant, and sometimes for no reason at all. These poor animals wander the streets looking for food and safety.

My mother always had two dogs in the house, and we were raised to love them like family. After she died, I took care of them until they passed away, and then my father didn't let me get another dog.

When I used to go to my mates' homes over long weekends, to a person, they had at least one family pet. I'm not in a position to get a dog now, so I thought I'd help save as many as I can. Most of the time, offers of food induce them into the car, but sometimes they're so scared they lash out, or run off.

After the first rescue, I had my car cleaned from top to bottom and learned my lesson. Now I have rubber coverings for the seats and there are two layers of blankets on top. Still, my car always smells like dog, but I don't mind.

I meant to ask in my last letter, were you able to compile your portfolio and put in your application to university to receive an early decision? I think you had mentioned two deadlines in regard to this process. Which did you choose, and when do you find out?

This is an exciting time in your life, and a first step to delving into your chosen area of study, as well as making new and lasting friendships. Get ready to spread your wings and fly.

Me

Di Caro Residence
The Studio
Sofia

No way was I able to make the Early Decision I deadline of November 1st. After being yanked back here in the middle of September, I need time to get my studio and my life back in order. I didn't want to rush putting my portfolio together since I had/have a few works in progress that I wanted to include if they came out good enough. I have to submit between fifteen and twenty works, and deciding, or curating if I want to sound chichi, which best represents me and my artistic vision, I opted for Early Decision II, which means I have to submit everything by January 1st. Now you know how exactly how I'm spending my winter break.

Before I forget, I wanted to tell you – dinner with Theresa was great. She talked about how much it helped her to get out of the house and return to normal routines. She was thrilled to go food shopping, and she spent forever walking around in the mall. What surprised me the most was how easy we were with each other. I thought being with her would make me feel guilty again, but seeing her eat and laugh helped lift the weight on my heart. We agreed to do it again soon.

So, after the dramarama of Thanksgiving, everything here is quiet, which is a relative term in this household. Exhibit A: the Christmas decorating frenzy has come and gone. Every year, the day after Thanksgiving the decorations start to go up, and by Sunday night, it's all done. My mother and Nonna expect everyone to participate. Well, except my father. He's not the climb on the ladder and string up the Christmas lights kind of guy. Duh. I'll start with the outside of the house and work my way in. Get out your mouthwash. Your teeth are going to ache from all the syrupy sweet.

The front of the house is where everything is understated and tasteful. Every tree that lines the circular drive at the front of the house is rigged with those teeny-tiny little white lights. I have to admit, it looks pretty and takes away the barren feel of the bare trees. On the front doors, we have two identical huge wreaths. Each year my mother goes with a theme, and this year it's a beach theme, which means we have blue and white coral and starfish, and tons of seashells. Some of the coral is glittered up, but, for the most part, my mother tones down the sparkle. She's good with color and choosing the right ribbons, ornaments, etc.

The wreaths on the door have starfish, small pieces of coral and seashells wired into big flowing ribbons that look like the ocean. Someone who does party stuff makes a lot of the decorations for Mom at her direction.

That's it for the front. Tree lights and wreaths.

Inside it's a Christmas explosion.

The entryway foyer has a twelve-foot tree. After the tree was erected – and I mean that literally since it's so big and heavy, it has steel supports going through this enormous tree stand – Gio's job is to hold the ladder. This year he loved his job since Nat went up and down the ladder the most. I know I don't need to explain why he loved it, do I? Nat didn't want Nonna anywhere near the ladder – that was a ten-minute argument, and can I mention, Nat is becoming a pro at getting her way and putting her foot down – and Mom wasn't allowed past the second step. Which meant everything from four feet and up, Nat hung on the tree. Half the time, she stayed on the ladder while we all argued about what should go where. That was the part Gio enjoyed the most. Again, for obvious reasons.

Dad hates having the banister wrapped, so Ro and I wrap the balusters. This year we had to be extra careful because each piece of thick blue ribbon had tiny seashells glued on. It took for-fucking-ever, and we lost a few shells, but it looks great.

Super-thick ribbons alternating starfish, coral, and seashells hang halfway down each wall of the hallway from a thin rail below the crown molding. The archways of each room have mistletoe hanging from them. Gio installs them and makes good use of their presence. Constantly. Ugh.

There's an eight-foot tree in the large dining room. That one was easy to decorate: it's all shiny blue and silver balls of various sizes with a giant starfish on top.

Then we decorate out back, and that's where the word ostentatious is explored to its outer limits. When we get done the yard looks garish, and I love it. Every tree around the patio and the pool house has little twinkly lights. The tree trunks are wrapped, too.

48

As I'm sure you guessed, we don't do the trees. My father's guys do. But we hang GIANT shiny balls from the lower branches and large twinkly snowflakes. The pool house is trimmed with white lights, and we have a life-size Santa sitting in his life-size sleigh on the roof. We have lighted reindeer all over the lawn – they're made of wrapped wire and are lit from nose to tail – and their heads move. Some look like they're grazing, some are upright. And, as if that weren't enough, we have two Christmas trees wrapped in twinkly lights with lighted snowflakes dangling from the branches on both sides of the pool house's French doors.

When it snows, the entire backyard glows.

The tree in the family room – another eight-footer – was the last thing we did, and we worked on it on Sunday. It took HOURS to decorate. This is the tree with all the family ornaments, and I confess, it's my fave. It's also the tree where the fighting is the loudest and fiercest. I'm beginning to wonder if I should switch profession choices and become an MLB referee. Trust me, nothing those damn Yankees could say would make a dent after growing up in this house.

At least Nonna was in the kitchen cooking while we were screaming at each other at the top of our lungs. Cooking didn't stop her from yelling too. Gio never gets into the arguments, and neither does Nat. When asked their opinions they give them, but if they're shot down, they shrug and chill while we kill each other over the placement of things like the little drummer boy Ro made when she was six.

Mom got us light blue stuffing stockings with white starfish on them with our names embroidered across the top in dark blue. Nat got a little teary when Mom handed hers over to hang off the fireplace mantel. Yet another excuse for Gio to hold Nat close and do that whispering thing for like a half-hour.

After all the tree drama, we go through the house, even upstairs, and strategically placing potpourri baskets, this time topped with seashells, coral and starfish that are trimmed with blue and white ribbons. When we were done, we were exhausted. Everyone cleaned up, changed clothes, came back downstairs, and couldn't wait to dig into dinner.

Dad comes in, makes a half-turn to take in the family room, then says, "Looks good, let's eat," and Ro and I looked at each other like are-you-fucking-kidding-me-right-now.

Miffy

Parisi Family Home
Vittoria, Sicily
Matteo

As she had been with him on that perfect night, her letters were enthusiastic and passionate in equal measure about her likes and dislikes. He thought back to when their night together went from being friendly to intimate.

"You never went home?" she asked, as if it were a felony.

"I did when I was at Eton, but only during the summer and most winter breaks."

"You were a kid. Thirteen." She looked at him with doe eyes. "That makes my heart hurt."

"Eons ago, and the way of things. Nobody whose family didn't live within a three-hour drive went home except for winter and spring break, and, of course, summer."

"How long?" He scrunched his brows so she clarified. "How long were the breaks?"

"Three weeks."

"What did you do for spring break if you didn't go home?"

"I went to one of my mate's house."

"I'm sorry. I don't want to speak badly about your father, but why didn't he bring you home?"

How did he explain his father's version of love when he had such a hard time understanding it himself? "My mother's death created problems he didn't anticipate."

She made a hand motion for him to continue.

"My father's interests took him to Naples and Rome often. My brothers took care of things here when he was gone. Watching over me, making sure I was attending to my studies, was not a priority."

"What the fuck?"

He laughed. She looked so delicate and fragile, but she had a mouth on her like a stevedore.

"No. Really. I get they didn't want to babysit you on Saturday night, but you're their brother. They should have been keeping you

close, especially because you were young and probably missed your mother in a more immediate way than they did."

"Perhaps. But it's not my father's way, and my brothers followed his lead."

"Excuse me for saying so, but his way sucks."

"He tried. For a while I was living with my mother's sister, my aunt Tina. But I was wild. I know now I behaved badly because of my mother's death, but at the time, I was difficult and was more of a handful than she wanted to take on. Her children were grown and had moved away. I don't fault her for not wanting to manage a headstrong twelve-year-old boy."

Sofia jerked her head back. *"Well, I do. Christ. You were a little boy who needed love and attention. Your family is supposed to give you that unconditionally."*

He knew better than to mention that she wanted to run away from all the love and attention she was getting fast. But he took her point. Somewhere between being suffocated and being abandoned there was a wide range of caring.

"I didn't turn out so bad."

"That's because of who you are, not what they did or, in this case, didn't do."

Since his mother died, Matteo couldn't recall anyone in his life having that kind of faith in him. Sofia barely knew him. But she believed in him. One month ago that would have been a boon to his ego and he would have considered waiting for this beautiful young woman to get a little older before seeing if they were as compatible as they seemed. Now? She would never know who he had to become and why. He would do anything and everything to ensure her safety, and for purely selfish reasons, he wanted her to remember him as she believed him to be.

"A kind sentiment. I'll remember that you thought so."

"Damn. They drilled the British understatement into you and good."

He chuckled. *"One doesn't emote in England, unless you're at a football game. Then, it's fitting to become barking mad."*

"I've heard about those games. You guys are worse than our football super fans. Beer and testosterone are not a good combination at a violent sporting event."

"Agreed."

"Do you play?"

"Recreationally."

"What about your brothers? You're grown now. Do you guys play together in neighborhood games?"

He'd been avoiding telling her, but there seemed no way around it. She'd get the story the family fabricated that was fed to everyone who wanted to know. Only a choice few people knew the truth, her father being one of them.

"My brothers are the reason I came home."

"How come?"

He lowered his voice and tried to say this as gently as possible. *"Because they died in a boating accident three weeks ago."*

Before he knew what she was about, she threw herself at him and wrapped her slender arms around his neck, pressing her forehead to his, their lips millimetres apart. In that moment he saw it in her eyes, she wanted him. *"Oh God. How horrible. I'm so, so sorry."* She squeezed him, gasped, then pulled back. *"Shit. I'm so sorry I said those things about them. Why didn't you shut me up?"*

With willpower he didn't know he had, gently, he pushed her back, creating an acceptable amount of space between them. For a moment his urge to kiss her, to wrap his arms around her and feel the press of her slight body against his was everything he wanted and needed, and he nearly gave in. Years of being the kid separated from his family, the child and brother who was more nuisance than the time it would have taken to love him, made Matteo vulnerable to her sweet compassion and fiery defense of his right to be cared for by his family.

But he knew better.

His mother raised him to be kind. Eton insisted he be a gentleman with impeccable manners. And the epically biblical retribution that would be exacted upon him by her father was enough to scare the shit out of the Royal Marines. Sofia talked about her father as a remote and controlling parent, but one involved in her life. Little did she know how powerful he was, and how feared for his swift justice.

"Because you were talking about how they behaved in the past, and their deaths didn't erase their prior actions."

Her shoulders slumped. "I guess." She drew in a deep breath. "I can't imagine how you feel, but I want you to know you can talk to me. I'm here for you."

Sofia would be so easy to love. A challenge to live with, but that meant he'd never get bored. She had a deep sense of loyalty that wouldn't waver. She'd stand by him in a way no one else ever had. In return, he would adore her for as long as she lived.

So stupid to fall for her, of all people. And right now, of all times, when he was forced to become something and someone he detested.

Why couldn't she be three years older, and why couldn't they have met years ago?

As Matteo stared at her letter, he had those same thoughts now as he'd had that night three months ago. But he'd made a promise to himself that he'd use the letters to guide her away from him. As much as he wanted to dive into the depths of her and swim in her wondrous soul, he had to push her toward a life that didn't include him.

Fuck.

Your vivid descriptions brought the decorations to life, and have forced me to reconsider my solo Christmas tree. I'm resolved to give it some sparkle.

I'm guessing Christmas will be equally noisy and boisterous, and that your nonna will make cucciddatini. I can eat two dozen of those cookies in one sitting. My father and I will be going to a cousin's home to celebrate, and much like your family, there will be a lot of people, all of whom have opinions they share loudly. My favorite part of the holiday is watching the small children open their presents. Catching the sheer joy when they get something they wished for, and the droopy faces when they receive clothes, or something practical, is priceless.

My best Christmas present was a bicycle my oldest brother, Due, gave me when I was eight. His real name was Edoardo. He was named after my father, and I guess they wanted to avoid confusion in the house. Since he was Edoardo the second, he became Due. Not a great nickname, but better than secondo. Could you imagine being called Condo your entire life?

I digress. Before that Christmas, I'd had a small bike and rode like a demon up and down the streets around our house. I fancied myself a future Tour de France contender. Due used to encourage me, and when he gave me the new bicycle, which wasn't a racing bike, but it was a ten-speed, every spare minute I had, I rode through the hills, building up my endurance.

Throughout most of the year there are pro races in Italy, and I'd thought if I got good enough to enter a race and do well, I could work my way up in the rankings and make it to the Tour de France. After my mother died, the bicycle became the means to alleviate frustration, and to get away from the house. When I started to ride too far, and come home too late, Due told me that our father was going to take the bike away if I didn't behave. In the riot of emotions of I was experiencing at eleven years old, the dream of cycling in Tour de France fell away.

I wasn't here to see it, but after forty-plus years of no official pro cycling in Sicily, the multi-day Giro della Sicilia came back this past April. The cyclists' route went along the coast, into mountain villages, and through the parks near Etna. I still cycle, and love to disappear for a couple of hours on my bike, but I couldn't compete with the pros. I'm damn good at weekend football matches, though. When I lived in London, I played regularly with a few of my former teammates from Eton.

Buon Natale, Miffy. My wish for you is to get into the programme you want at university, and that you follow your dreams. You deserve to lead a full and happy life.

Me

Di Caro Residence
The Studio
Sofia

What the fuck? *I deserve to lead a full and happy life.* Who was he talking to, a stranger?

That letter was off. On the one hand he told a couple of personal stories, and on the other it felt like he thought about every word he wrote. Maybe she *should* buy a burner phone. She could get Ro to go shopping with her, Mom, and *Nonna*, and use her cranky sister as a distraction while she slipped away.

Right. Like that was even a remote possibility. Two of Dad's "men" followed them everywhere, and *Nonna* had eyes in the back of her head and the vision of a hawk.

Dammit. Sofia needed to talk to Matteo. Bad.

The next day, Sofia sat down next to Amy in the cafeteria. "You have to tell me if I'm crazy."

"You're fuckin' nuts. I love you, but you're off your mind."

"Ha. Ha." Sofia pulled Matteo's latest letter out of her backpack. "Read this. Don't say a word until I ask my question."

Amy held out her hand, bent her head, and got to reading. A couple of minutes later, she looked up and waited for Sofia to ask, "Does it sound off?"

"Off. As in not correct?"

"Off as in impersonal."

Amy sighed, put her hand over Sofia's, and said, "It sounds like he's a wonderful man trying to be a nice guy."

Sofia felt the sting in her nose and forced back the tears. "Then what the fuck?" she whispered.

"Soph." Amy squeezed Sofia's fingers. "He's thousands of miles away, and he's twenty-two years old. No doubt you shared a wonderful few hours and made a connection. If he didn't feel it too, he wouldn't've bothered doing the whole TLC thing with you. But you have to be realistic. What did you think would come of this?"

Sofia sniffed and pulled her hand out from under Amy's and balled it in her lap. "I thought we'd deepen the 'connection' and when I turned eighteen, I'd go to Sicily for the summer and spend as much time with him as I could before I came back to go to college."

"Does he know that?"

Sofia shrugged. "It was implied."

Amy laughed. "Soph. You're too sweet." Sofia got ready to respond, but Amy kept talking. "No. Really. You need to be an artist when you're doing your art. I get that. But the rest of the time, you can't be all sensitive and giving to every guy who smiles at you."

"That's bullshit, Ames. I don't do that, and you know it. Lemme list all the guys I didn't even let get past, 'Hey, babe.'"

"Okay. Okay. Let me rephrase. When you like a guy, you're kinda blind to who they are."

"Don't you dare use Walter against me."

"I'm not. I was thinking of Todd Piniack."

Sofia blinked a few times. "Todd? What about him?"

"He wasn't exactly a true-blue kind of guy."

"So I noticed."

"*After* he lied to you about like four other girls."

"Now you're being mean."

"No. I'm saying you're sweet. You want to believe the best in people. It's an admirable trait, but it leads you to the kind of disappointment you're feeling now."

Sofia dipped her head. "Matt's not like other guys. I know you don't believe me, or think I'm making more out of that night than what really happened, but I swear, Ames, he's the one. I know it." She raised her head. "I'm not being all dreamy. He felt it too. You should have heard him when we spoke on Halloween. I was crying in that bathroom as much for him as me. I heard the hurt in his voice."

Amy sighed. "Okay, Soph. Let's say you're right. No reason not to lay it out for him. Tell him about what you expect to happen this summer. If he's down with it, there's your answer." Amy leaned in so her face was inches away from Sofia's. "But if he's not, you end it. Clean break. He's right. You should follow your dreams. You deserve to live a full and happy life with someone who thinks you walk on water and will do everything to protect that sweet heart of yours."

Sofia couldn't help the tears that rolled down her face or talk past the knot in her throat. So she nodded.

"Promise me, Soph." Amy grabbed Sofia's shoulders and shook. "Promise me."

Sofia gulped. "I promise, Ames."

That night, Sofia called Theresa and they agreed it was a good idea to meet for dinner the next day.

Stavaros Greek Restaurant
Dutchford
Sofia

"I didn't know this was here."

Theresa had already taken her seat at their table, but Sofia was still standing looking around the restaurant at all the murals of the Greek Islands.

"They opened about three months ago. I've heard good things so I thought we'd try it."

Sofia sat. "*Nonna* told me if a restaurant is busy in the middle of the week it means they'll stay in business." Sofia saw only two empty tables. "I think you made a good choice."

"I hope so. I'm hungry." Theresa opened her menu.

Sofia didn't know if she should say she noticed Theresa was putting back some of the weight she'd lost. Those kind of conversations were tricky. In the interest of avoiding fucking up, Sofia held her tongue. "I don't know a lot about Greek food. What do you recommend?"

Theresa rattled off a bunch of dishes, then suggested they share the sampling plate. Not knowing *saganaki* from *spanakopita,* Sofia agreed, and felt stupid. "You know, I'm realizing I don't know much about food outside of basic American stuff, and, of course, all things Italian."

"Pretty typical for someone your age who didn't grow up in a city." Theresa ripped a bread pocket in half, pointed to some creamy-looking stuff with orange something or other sprinkled over the top, and said, "Take some hummus and put it on your plate, then dip a piece of pita into it. I think you'll like it."

Sofia was game and did as Theresa suggested. Yummmm. "What did you call this?"

"Hummus. It's ground-up chickpeas with olive oil and garlic."

"*Ceci* beans? Really?"

Theresa laughed. "Really. Greek food is Mediterranean food also."

"God. I love *panelle*. *Nonna* makes it all the time. There were these street vendors in Sicily that sold *panelle*, and it tasted fabulous."

"See? Not such a limited palate after all. Many Mediterranean dishes are similar with different names depending on the country or culture. My guess, you'll love Greek food, and maybe you'll even bring your *nonna* here."

"Ha. *Nonna* doesn't think anyone cooks as good as she does. She's a restaurant snob."

"Maybe if you boast about how delicious the food is here, she'll be tempted to come to see for herself."

"You're sneaky." Theresa grinned. "You used to do sneaky things to get me to talk. I didn't notice at the time, but afterwards, I figured out how you got me to spill."

"Do I need to be sneaky tonight, or are you going to 'spill' on your own?"

Sofia wanted to hide. She hated being so transparent. "You know I'd be happy being with you if we only talked about *The Bachelorette*."

Theresa smiled. "I know. And we can do that if you want."

"See?" Sofia wagged her finger. "Sneaky."

The waitress brought the most enormous platter Sofia had ever seen outside her house. Much like *Nonna*'s overstuffed antipasti plate, this ginormo platter was filled to the brim with wondrous-smelling food.

"Holy shit," Sofia whispered when the waitress left. "We're going to be sampling for hours."

Theresa laughed then started to explain what all the food was. Sofia couldn't remember the name of everything, but damn, it all tasted fantastic.

While they ate, they talked about *The Bachelorette*. When they'd had their fill, the waitress took the platter away to make up a take-home box for Theresa. Sofia gave herself a mental kick in the ass, and took a deep breath before asking, "Do you think I'm blind to who the guys really are? I mean the ones I like. And don't ask me what I think. Tell me what you think."

Theresa dabbed her mouth with her napkin, then placed it back in her lap. "I think you want your relationships with guys to go smoothly, and when they display behavior that rocks the boat, you gloss over what they're doing and why."

Shit. Maybe Sofia shouldn't've insisted. Then she stopped herself from going down the pity trail and thought about what Theresa said. And thought some more. Then her hands began to shake, and she pushed them underneath her thighs. Fuck. Now Sofia felt like she'd been smacked between the eyes for an entirely different reason. "Oh. My. God. You just described how my mother is with my father."

Theresa raised her brows, which Sofia knew meant, "Go on."

"They don't fight. Well, they don't fight in front of us, but really, I don't think they fight. She does whatever he wants, and he treats her like she's the most wonderful person in the world."

Theresa sat back in her chair and waited silently. Sofia knew what that meant too. Theresa was giving Sofia space to find her way to an answer.

"I didn't fight with the guys I dated because I wanted them to treat me like I'm the most wonderful person in the world." Sofia shook her head. "I'm an idiot."

Theresa leaned forward and said, "Far from it. There isn't a human being alive who doesn't want the person they love, or like, to think they're wonderful. And if you choose well, they do, about half the time. The other half, they get angry with you for all sorts of reasons big and small. Or they had a bad day and you're the person they dump it on, right or wrong. Or. Or. Or. We can adore someone and still get pissed off at them. If the relationship is strong, you fight it out until you get to a place somewhere in the middle."

Sofia thought of Gio and Nat. "My future sister-in-law has no problem arguing with my brother. On Christmas Day, when everyone was downstairs, they didn't know I was in the upstairs hall and boy were they going at it. I went down the back staircase so they wouldn't hear me leave. Half hour later, they come strolling into the family room, my brother's arm around Nat's shoulders, her arm around Gio's waist with her thumb in his belt loop and her hand in his back pocket. I nearly fell over. I'd thought they were breaking up they were so intense when they were fighting."

"Sounds like they're passionate people who have a strong bond. People who know that about their relationship aren't afraid to argue."

"Most of the time, they're pretty nauseating. They're so into each other they don't even try to curtail the PDA."

Theresa laughed. "Get used to it. If I had to guess, they're going to be that way their whole lives."

"Ugh."

The waitress came over and asked if they wanted dessert. Sofia looked at the woman like she'd lost her mind.

When they were outside the coatroom, Theresa told Sofia, "Whatever it is you feel you need to say to Matteo, say it, even if it leads to an argument. How you fight is as important as how you express your love. Sometimes, more important."

Sofia asked, "Is it okay if I hug you?"

Theresa smiled and said, "It's more than okay."

Sofia held on way longer than she expected.

Di Caro Residence
Sofia's Bedroom
Sofia

She'd been lying on her bed staring at the ceiling for a while now. She couldn't shake the realization that she'd been behaving like her mother. Sofia adored her mom. The woman devoted herself to her family completely. She gave the best hugs, never yelled at her kids – well, she yelled the way everyone in the house did like when they decorated for Christmas, but she never yelled in anger – and she made sure everyone knew they were loved. But Sofia didn't want the kind of marriage her mother had, and couldn't imagine doing everything her husband wanted the way her mother catered to Dad.

While Sofia wasn't a fan of confrontation, she hadn't thought of herself as someone who would acquiesce to her man about everything. But as she reviewed her past relationships, she began to see that when push came to shove, she gave in. If the guy she'd been dating wanted to eat at a burger joint when she wanted Chinese food, they ate at a burger joint. If he wanted to see a bang-bang shoot-'em-up movie, that's what they saw. At the time, she hadn't given it much thought, but in retrospect, she hadn't stood up for what she wanted because she didn't want the guy to think she was difficult. How she had equated saying she preferred to eat in a Chinese restaurant was being difficult became clear when Theresa pushed her into taking a hard look at herself. Sofia didn't like what she saw.

But… One of the reasons she'd felt so comfortable with Matteo was because she had argued with him, and he had liked it.

"Where do you prefer to live, England or here?" Sofia asked. They'd moved off the rocks and were walking down the lane, the moon still shining, but it had dropped farther into the western sky.

"I have a flat in London. That's my home now. I prefer the weather here in the winter, but my life philosophy is more in keeping with the British. No doubt because I was schooled there during the most important years of my formal learning."

"You certainly act more British than Sicilian. Doesn't all that restraint exhaust you?"

He laughed. "*You Yanks think saying whatever is on your mind is some sort of badge of honor. It's as if no one understands least said soonest mended.*"

"*Ha. This from a country where gossip has been an industry for hundreds of years.*"

"*Perhaps in the media, but in private lives, being circumspect shows consideration for other people's feeling. You don't have to share every thought that passes through your brain.*"

"*Better to be repressed then?*"

"*Not repressed. Exercising self-control.*"

"*Holy shit. All that self-control will give you a heart attack. You have to let your feelings out. Isn't it you guys who say better out than in?*"

"*Yes, but it doesn't extend to sharing bathroom habits. You lot don't have filters.*"

"*I'd rather deal with someone who lets me know what they're thinking and feeling than trying to guess what some vague comment or pursed lips might mean. You're Italian. Sicilian. Doesn't your family yell and scream and carry on over every little thing?*"

He shook his head. "*We can be noisy. And some members of the family are given to more drama than is necessary, but we do not 'carry on.' It's bad form.*"

"*Jesus.*" She couldn't help it. She started laughing and couldn't stop. "*Bad form,*" she sputtered.

Matteo grinned when she bent at the waist holding her side. "*I'm glad you find me amusing.*"

She wiped her eyes and shook her head. "*I think you're full of shit.*"

"*That.*" He pointed at her. "*That right there is exactly what I'm talking about. I got from your case of the giggles that you didn't agree with me. But to tell me I'm full of shit because we approach things differently is, quite frankly, offensive.*"

She started laughing again. "*You're...offended?*"

He put his hands on his hips and scowled. "*Not in the least. I was making a point.*"

"*The point, prince charming, is that people need to be honest about how they feel. All this hiding behind 'self-control' is a great way to avoid dealing. You don't strike me as a guy who doesn't step up.*"

"I'll take that as a compliment."

"It was meant as one."

He smiled. "You're feisty."

"Can you handle it?"

He leaned in and lowered his voice. "Most definitely, little rabbit."

Sofia left her bedroom and went downstairs to her studio.

Let's see if he can really handle it.

Happy New Year! I can't believe the holidays have come and gone. Since I'm counting the days until I graduate and turn eighteen, time has been mostly dragging. Having Nat and Gio here has made the past couple of weeks fly by. They're gone now. Flew out yesterday to spend about thirteen days in Fiddlers Rest, this little town where Nat used to live when she and Gio started writing to each other through The Letter Club. She loves the town and the people she worked with. He spent last summer there with her and said everyone treated him like family. They made friends I think will last a lifetime.

I had dinner with Theresa earlier this evening. She's doing great and she took me to a new Greek restaurant in town. The food was soooo good. I ate until I couldn't move. Definitely, I'll be going back there. Soon.

Before I forget, Akiva's bar mitzvah was great. Low dramarama, especially for us. Aunt Toni is clever. Instead of grouping all Aaron's family at their own tables, and all our family on the other side of the room at our tables, which is what Mom would've done, Toni mixed us up. For most of our family that was an enormous neon sign that warned in flashing lights they had to be on their best behavior. NO WAY would they want to be talked about badly by another family. Blended tables meant civilized dinner conversation. See, clever Toni.

As I'd mentioned, Toni, Aaron and their tribe live in a big, old farmhouse. And they have acreage. They plant a lot of their food in this amazing garden, and they have a meadow, and a small creek that runs through a little forest of their own. Most of the time they have parties in a giant tent in the meadow. With their huge, ginormo family, it's the sane thing to do and keeps everyone from climbing the walls. But it's been really cold, and we've had a couple of early snows, so after we left the synagogue – can I take a minute to tell you how composed Nonna tried to be during services? It's not like she hasn't been through this before with Adam and Abe, but every time they read from the Torah in Hebrew, she makes this face like she can't believe a relative of hers isn't speaking English or Italian. Since this was Nat's first time at a family bar mitzvah, she caught Nonna's expression and nearly fell over from keeping in her laughter. Gio kept pinching her to keep her from letting it go. That alone had me shaking with silent laughter. Don't think my father didn't catch the whole thing, he did, but his lips twitched like he wanted to bust out laughing too.

After we left the synagogue, we went to this modern, upscale, two-story restaurant overlooking the Hudson River. Toni and Aaron rented out the whole place. After dinner, there was a DJ, and we danced for hours. Almost everyone stayed the night at this nice hotel near the restaurant. You should've seen us the next morning at the buffet breakfast. Swarmed by our noisy family, the hotel staff looked like they'd been hit by a tornado. Which they had.

It's been a week since I've been back at school, and I feel like I'm biding time. Most of the seniors feel that way since we're all waiting to hear where we got in, and then it's cruising 'til graduation. I applied to three other universities as backup if I don't get into Tufts. Northeastern because they have the College of Arts and Media Design. Rhode Island School of Design because they are art centric, plus they're down the hill from Brown, so for a year I'd have Gio and Nat nearby. And Massachusetts College of Art and Design, who were almost my first choice. They're well regarded and have a great program, but Tufts is a step above.

My BF applied to Boston University and Northeastern, and that's it. She'll get into both, she's super smart. BU is her first choice. I'd like to have her nearby. We've been friends since sixth grade and it'll be weird not seeing her every day, but if she and I are in Boston, we'll get to be together whenever we can.

One of the many things I've been doing as I'm getting mentally ready to head off to college is planning for the summer. I've decided to go back to Sicily so I can spend time with you. Once the fall semester starts, I'm going to be inundated with work. It's not the academics I'm worried about. It's my art. Right now I'm in a world of my own, where I'm the judge of whether I'm measuring up to my standards. Once I get into one of the university programs, my art will be judged by people who do that for a living. It's not the scrutiny that worries me, it's making sure no one tries to compromise my vision. I'm hoping for guidance that leads to a deeper understanding of my art, not a dictator who expects me to follow their artistic directive.

Heading to bed now.

Miffy

Parisi Family Home
Vittoria, Sicily
Matteo

Fuck. He threw Sofia's letter on his bed and cursed himself. *This is all my fucking fault. I let things go too far.* He hadn't meant to, but that night months ago, that bloody perfect night, which should have never happened, he had shown her his heart, and then handed it to her on a goddamn silver platter.

They had wandered about halfway down the road when Sofia motioned for him to follow her on a narrow path through the Aleppo pine. Matteo's family home was on the north side of the city. He wasn't familiar with the off-road pathways south of town, so he relied on her as she zigzagged through the trees. After about five minutes, she turned left and went down a small grade that took them to a narrow but steady flowing stream surrounded by large stones.

"How did you find this place?"

"Pretty cool, huh?"

He nodded.

"I'm bored to tears, literally, so when I sneak out, I explore. And before you start lecturing me about how it isn't safe, do you really think someone is going to come around Enzo's property with all those guards who roam everywhere all the time while toting guns?"

Matteo sighed. "Miff." She scrunched her nose without realizing she was doing the little rabbit thing he adored. "Let's sit." He waited until she found two large stones side by side, then she sat and looked up at him.

Sweet Christ. The trust shining from her pale blue eyes made him want to get down on his knees and beg her to forget she ever met him. He wasn't worthy of that trust. Well, maybe he was today, but in a few short months, he would be a man she would despise. If she knew what he was going to do, she'd walk away from him right now. He couldn't tell her, but he wished there was a way to let her know who and what he was about to become.

"Listen to me, and please, take what I'm saying to heart. There are people who would gladly risk their lives to kidnap you. If for no

other reason than to have fleeting bragging rights that they got one over on your father." She scowled. "Some of those people would kill you and dump you on Enzo's doorstep. And some would do so much worse until you'd wish you were dead. Do you understand me?"

"I'm not oblivious, Matt. I know who my father is and what he does. Maybe not all he does, but enough to know that we are not your average suburban family. Huge house and money aside, how long do you think it took me to figure out my family was different? Try the first grade. What was I? Six?

"Everyone in our class was invited to this girl's birthday party. It was the first time I went to anyone else's house. My mother came with me, and you know what question number one was when we pulled into the girl's driveway?" Matteo knew where this was going but waited for her continue. "Where are the gates and the men to protect the house?" She glared at him as if it was his fault. "My mother's answer was something like, 'Not everyone has the same kind of security systems in their house. Some you can't see.' I remember spending the entire party looking for something or someone that showed me this family had security. No shit. Other kids were playing pin-the-tail-on-the-donkey and I was worried about bad people coming over and ruining the party because I couldn't find the security."

"We grew up with different realities, Sofia. Why do you think I live in London?"

"You're old enough to do that for yourself, plus you're a guy. Gio always had beaucoup freedom compared to me and Ro." He tilted his head in question. "My younger sister, Aurora."

"Your father's parents were born here, and they were raised by people whose families have lived here for eons. Everything they knew and believed they had to have shared with him. That's his frame of reference, right or wrong."

"It's all fucking wrong. I may not look like much, but I'm committed to my art and I'll plow down anyone who tries to sidetrack me from making that my life's work."

"Back up. What do you mean you 'may not look like much'?"

She motioned from her head down her body. "Gio is so gorgeous women in the supermarket trip over their feet when they see him. News flash. He's the younger version of my father. My mother is stunning. Still. Ro is the perfect combination of both our parents, and she's no skinny little waif-looking thing. Me, I have thin, wispy, nondescript brown hair, washed-out blue eyes, and I have the body of an eight-year-old boy." She put her hands over her tiny breasts. "No tits." She moved her hands to her hips. "From my rib cage down, there are no curves, and believe me when I tell you, my ass is pretty much nonexistent."

Matteo's mouth opened and he committed a cardinal sin. He didn't exercise judgment. He didn't stop to consider the impact of his words. He spoke the truth straight from his heart. "You are so wrong. You're lovely. Ethereal. Your passion shines out of you, creating a bright light everyone is drawn to. You're brutally honest, yet unbelievably compassionate. While you'll probably hate me for saying this, I understand why your father wants to wrap you in cotton batting. You're precious and rare. He'd be a fool if he didn't protect you the way he does."

Her eyes glittered with unshed tears, which tore at his soul. And made him more stupid than he'd been already. He reached out and took both her small, delicate hands in his. "From now on, you must promise me you'll cry only happy tears. I know right now your life is not what you want it to be, but trust me, it will be. You'll return home, and your friends, family, and your art will be there, waiting for you. My loss will be tempered by the knowledge that you're happy and carrying on. Which you will because you have an indomitable spirit."

Gently, he squeezed her hands. "Let's get you back to your uncle's house," Matteo looked up at the lightening sky, "before sunrise."

Happy New Year to you too, albeit belated. Of the many things I wish for you, getting into Tufts is the top of the list. I'm glad to hear Akiva's bar mitzvah went well. It seems your aunt equals your grandmother in having a tactical mind and a general's maneuvers. Important skills with an unwieldy family.

Unfortunately, I won't be in Sicily this summer. My work will take me around the world, and as of now, I can't say where I'll be when. I'm sure Enzo, Valentina, and Mia would love to see you, but I would have thought you'd like to go somewhere new before you start university. Once your classes begin, you'll have little time for socializing, and given the nature of your studies, I imagine you'll be spending much of your day creating your art.

Since I've travelled a bit more than you, I have a suggestion: Canada is lovely in the summer and far cooler than the Mediterranean. Perhaps you and your best friend would like to do a four-city tour, starting in Montreal, which is as close to France as you can get in North America. The food is divine, and by new world standards, the city boasts a rich history. I had the good fortune to visit a mate from Eton who was studying at McGill University. His family is from the city, and I was treated to the best kind of tour guide: a homegrown one. While I haven't been to Toronto, or anywhere else in Canada, I understand it's a world-class city, much on par with New York City. Since you like city life, I imagine you'd find Toronto fascinating.

I've heard Calgary is Canada's version of Texas, full of cowboys, rodeos, and oil. While not my usual entertainment, I think it would be fun to see the city and take in its flavor. Artists benefit from exposing themselves to different sensory input. My guess, you'll get a kick out of visiting there.

The place in Canada I'd like to go next is Vancouver. I've heard it's beautiful, and a bit like being in Seattle, but nicer and less harried because everyone is Canadian. If you took the four-city tour, you could end in Vancouver, or drop down to Seattle before heading home.

Whatever you choose to do, and wherever you decide to go, I'm sure you'll have a great time.

Fingers crossed you get a thumbs-up from Tufts soon.

Me

It had taken Matteo four hours to write that horrid letter. There was no good way to tell Sofia not to come visit him. Who the hell knew what his life would be like five months from now? Of one thing he was certain: it wouldn't resemble anything he'd want to subject her to. Also, he didn't want her here. It wasn't safe for her in Sicily, even if everything wasn't fucked up.

If she persisted, he'd have to tell her father.

And then she'd surely hate him.

Better that than any chance she'd be in harm's way.

She was young. She'd get over her disappointment and move on with her life. She'd find someone worthy of her love, passion, and loyalty.

And if he was alive when she hitched herself to whoever that motherfucker turned out to be, Matteo would make certain that fucker treated Sofia like the most precious thing on earth.

Because she was.

Di Caro Residence
The Studio
Sofia

Waiting wasn't Sofia's strong suit. When she was a little kid, her mother always told Ro, who – surprise, surprise – acted out all the time, "Look at how well your sister is waiting. You need to learn to be patient, like Sofia."

Ha. Sofia wasn't patient. She'd become a master at covering what she was thinking and feeling. Her parents thought she was the model of grace and ease. Inside she was throwing open doors and running through them as fast as her feet could take her.

Stupid, really, not to let her family know who she was and what she truly wanted. But from an early age, she'd learned pretending to be docile got her more of what she desired, and sooner. Inadvertently, her parents had taught her to be a chameleon. And a charlatan. Not the life lessons they were going for, huh?

Two things had her climbing the walls. First, Amy hadn't been in school for two days. Begging to use the phone at home was out of the question, so Sophia got creative. She went into the school's main office and told one of the secretaries that she lost a paper she needed to work on, and she thought it was at Amy's house, but since they weren't allowed to have phones in school, and Amy was home sick, Sofia needed to call Amy to find out if the paper was there so someone could pick it up for her.

The secretary, who knew Sofia was a "good kid" because she never came into the office for any reason, said yes immediately, and dialed Amy's number, then handed the handset to Sofia.

See, the docile charlatan was a good gig. Dishonest, but effective.

"Hello," Amy coughed into the phone. Shit. Sofia was right. Amy *was* sick.

"Hi, Ames. I'm in the main office, and they let me call you to find out if I left my English paper at your house."

Amy, who'd played many emotional scams with Sofia, caught on right away. "I'm so sorry, Soph. The paper isn't here." Code for no letter from Matteo. Dammit.

"How are you feeling?" That was a real question asked with genuine concern.

"Like shit. It's been wicked cold, you know, and like an idiot, I went out to get nail polish at Walgreens and left the house without my coat. I thought I'd be in the street for like two minutes. To the store and back. But Monica called when I was out and asked me to stop at like fifteen places. Need I say," she coughed and wheezed, "more?"

Sofia shook her head. "No. Stop talking and get better."

"I'll be back as soon as I can. Promise."

"Rest, Ames."

"Right." She hung up, coughing.

Sofia handed the receiver to the secretary, who looked at her like she was the sweetest kid in the world. "Thanks."

"You're welcome, dear. I hope Amy gets well soon."

"Me too," Sofia mumbled.

That was two days ago. Tomorrow was Friday. If Amy didn't come to school tomorrow, Sofia was stuck waiting another three days for Matt's letter. If it'd even come. Shitty to be thinking about that knowing Amy was home sick. If Sofia had normal parents, who led normal lives, she would have her phone. Enough said on that topic.

The second thing that had her jumping out of her skin was no word from Tufts. She'd gotten into Rhode Island School of Design, which was great, but not the awesome Tufts would be. Her parents were thrilled because if she went to RISD she would be close to Brown, which meant close to Gio, which *really* meant another set of eyes and ears keeping track of her. Not that Gio was like that, far from it, but that was definitely the way their father thought. Plus, Providence was a much smaller city than Boston, and the 'rents were all about "living in a safe environment conducive to learning," and according to them, Providence offered her that safety more than Boston.

Good thing she'd had years of practice keeping her shit under wraps, 'cause every time they said that or something like it, she wanted to gag. Or hurl. Sometimes both.

Four months and one day until her eighteenth birthday. She could almost taste the freedom. The day after she turned legal, she was boarding a plane for Sicily, and the first thing she was going to do after she cleared customs was lay a deep, wet, full-of-tongues, long, long kiss on Matteo's sexy mouth. Then she was going to get to the bottom of what was eating him.

She remembered how damn close her lips had been to his that night. She still couldn't believe he hadn't closed the tiny gap between them and taken what she had been so willing to offer.

She'd led the way out of the woods, and they walked down to the road that went past Enzo's house. As they got closer to the hedge, Matteo took her hand in his, and she near fell over. The moment their skin touched she got a shock as if he'd sent her an electrical jolt. Sort of like when she walked in her socks across the rug in her bedroom and touched the door handle. Zing, snap, sizzle. Except the zing didn't stop in her hand. Oh no, that current travelled around her nipples, down into her stomach, then took a deep dive and hit her clit, making her wet and ready.

She knew he felt it too because he stumbled a bit, stopped short, then turned to look at her, and holy shit, those caramel coffee eyes were on fire.

"Matt," she whispered.

He shook his head. "Don't."

"But —"

"I'm twenty seconds away from committing a crime. Help me not do that."

She nodded, then pulled her hand out of his.

His chin lowered and he closed his eyes. "Would that I could..."

"What?" He'd mumbled and she barely heard him.

He opened his eyes and bent down so they were at eye level. "If you remember nothing else about this night, remember this: Everything I didn't do was for you." Before she could ask what he meant, he tilted his head toward the house and said, "Go."

She wanted to lay her cheek against his broad chest and burrow in. She wanted to kiss him. Hug him. Hold on to him and never let go. But she saw the determination in the jut of his jaw and figured she'd go for now, but tomorrow they'd talk. Find a way to make this work.

She stretched up and whispered in his ear, "G'night, Matt."
Then, without looking back, she walked to the hedge and pushed
through, knowing he was watching her.

She should have looked back.

The next twenty-four hours were the worst of her life.

She snuck in through the "servant's entrance," which led into
the kitchen. Then she rounded the corner to take the back stairway
up to her room when Cro-Magnon man one, Aldo, grabbed her by
the upper arm and pulled her down the hall to the front of the house.

"Hey." She tried to pull her arm away.

He stared at her and didn't let go. Then he moved them to the
formal staircase and yelled up in Italian, "Got her, boss."

Shit. They'd found out she had "escaped."

When Enzo made the turn to the landing, he lifted his chin and
Aldo let her go. "Come upstairs, Sofia." She turned and glared at
Aldo, turned back and went up the stairs, passing her cousin on the
landing. She walked down the long hallway to her bedroom, went in,
stood by the window, and crossed her arms over her chest. Enzo
came in, closed the door, and sat at the end of her bed.

"Where were you, cara?"

"Out walking."

"Until," he tilted his head at the window, "sunrise."

"Yep."

"I'm guessing you weren't alone."

"Nope."

"Who is he?"

"A friend of the family's."

"No friend of our family would keep a teenage girl out all
night."*

Sofia sighed. She wanted to tell him she was going to be eighteen
in a few months, but knowing how the Sicilians thought, she figured
it would fall on deaf ears. "Listen, it's no big deal. We walked and
talked. That's it." She moved her hand down her body then re-
crossed her arms. "I'm fine. It's all good. Let's not make a big thing
out of it."

"I'm afraid it is a big thing, cara. Every night, before I go to bed,
I check to make sure everyone is safe in their rooms. When I didn't
see you in your bed, I searched the house, then tracked your phone.
When I found it here," he pointed to the nightstand drawer, "I went

to Mia and asked if she knew where you were. When she told me she didn't, immediately, I sent the guards out looking for you. Then, as I was getting ready to call your father, he called me."

Oh shit. Bad turned to the absolute worse in a heartbeat.

"Exactly." Enzo had read her expression. "Your father asked if Matteo Parisi had been to the house. I figured you were with Matteo, and told your father you were missing, but I felt certain we would find you, and that I'd call him as soon as we did. Right now, he's somewhere over the Atlantic on his way here. He knows you're safe, but he's concerned. I expect he'll arrive at the house around three this afternoon."

Sofia drew in a long breath through her nose.

When she didn't respond to him – like she had anything to say about all the shit that was about to descend on her head – he said, "Since you didn't sleep last night, you won't be going to school today. Try to rest."

She stared at him and wondered if he'd lost his mind. Her father was on his way, which meant she had to call Matteo ten minutes ago and tell him to leave Sicily right now.

As if he'd read her mind, Enzo said, "I have your phone. If you need anything, let Valentina know. She'll be staying home with us."

Fan-fucking-tastic. He was guilting her while letting her know she was more a prisoner than she had been seven hours ago. Since she had no options, and she sure as hell had nothing to say, she nodded.

Enzo stood and motioned to the bed. "Sleep, cara.*" Then he left.*

Ten minutes later, Sofia was standing where she had been during the Enzo lecture, still staring at the closed bedroom door. When it opened, she nearly jumped out of her skin. Mia came into the room, looking worried. Now Sofia felt double guilt on top of nausea.

Mia wrapped her arms around Sofia and whispered in Italian, "I wish I'd known."

Sofia stepped back, keeping the Italian going since Mia thought her English wasn't the greatest. "Known what?"

"About you and Matteo."

Huh? Until a few hours ago there was no Sofia and Matteo. "I barely know him." Sort of true, but mostly a lie.

"Well then," Mia said as if she was stating the obvious. "What were you doing with him all night long?"

Oh Christ. Mia thought the same thing her father did, and, more importantly, the same thing Sofia's father had to be thinking. "It wasn't like that. We didn't sleep together. We walked around here," she threw her arm out toward the window that opened to the formal gardens, "and talked. That's all."

"You don't have to practice your story on me," she huffed.

Sofia wanted to stomp her foot and scream. Instead she murmured, "Think what you want. I'm tired, and you have to get to school." Sofia kissed Mia on the cheek. "See you later."

Mia tilted her head like she was trying to read the truth on Sofia's face. "Okay," Mia said. "I'll bring your assignments home."

Sofia nodded and Mia left.

Knowing that encounter was the tip of a glacier-size iceberg careening across the Atlantic, Sofia's body gave off a full-blown exhaustion notice. She knew she'd need her all her strength for when her father arrived. Actually, she needed Thor's hammer. Sighing, she shed her clothes, pulled on one of Gio's old Brown University long-sleeve tees, climbed into bed, and stared at the ceiling, praying her father didn't kill Matteo.

Somehow, in the middle of all that praying, she fell asleep.

***

She felt the bed depress and forced her lids open. Her father, his face soft, his eyes warm with love, was leaning over her. She blinked a few times to clear away the cobwebs, certain she was dreaming. Her father never *looked at her like that.*

By the time she was fully awake, his face was a mask of impassivity.

That she recognized.

She pushed up until her back was against the headboard. "Hey, Dad."

"Sofia."

"I know you're quantum pissed off, and I get it, but you have to listen to me. We walked and talked, that's it. He didn't kiss me, or anything like that. He's a good guy." Her father's jaw muscle twitched. "No, really. I told him I went out walking alone at midnight." Now his face looked like thunder. "And he didn't want me wandering alone. He told me it was dangerous, and he kept me

company to keep me safe." Well, she didn't know if all that was true, but Matt had given her the safety lecture.

When her father didn't say anything but continued with his assessing glare, she lost her temper and hissed at him, "If it'll make you feel better, let's go to a doctor right now. Then after you find out I'm telling you the truth, I expect you to apologize."

One brow went up and he gave her a half grin. "When negotiating a position, it's wise not to give it all away at once, and it's definitely unwise to rub your opponent's nose in his defeat before it's fait accompli.*"*

"Are you my opponent, Dad?"

"Never," he stated firmly. "But the whole flight over I wondered if you had a death wish."

She drew in her breath so swiftly she double gasped. "You can't believe I wanted Walter to shoot me."

"That pezzo di merda *hadn't even crossed my mind."*

Well. That's better. And he was right. Walter was a piece of shit. "I don't understand. Explain."

"At first, bringing you here was to get you away from everything that had happened. But leaving you here was my way of giving you time to heal and live somewhere safe where you could be...you. Then I find out you're wandering around alone in the middle of the night." He glared at her, and on anyone else, a glare conveyed dissatisfaction, even anger. Her father's glare was a honed nuclear explosion.

She wasn't going to get into the wandering alone and the safety talk. She'd never win that argument and she was smart enough not to bother trying. "Dad, I don't even have a studio here. How can I be me if I don't have my art?"

He sighed. He knew she'd sidestepped the most important parts of his statement, and he was letting her dodge his bullet. "My apologies. I hadn't thought of that. An oversight I regret."

"Are you going to ask Enzo if it's okay I turn one of the rooms into my studio?"

"No. We're going home."

Now she had whiplash. He wanted her here, but he was taking her home. Only one thought popped into her head. Holy shit. Matteo was dead already.

"Ah. Why?"

"Because you're not safe here."

"Matteo would never hurt me."

"Not directly."

Okay, that answer indicated Matt was still alive.

"What does that mean?"

"It means there are things you don't know and never will."

"About him?"

He shook his head. Once.

"His family."

He dipped his chin.

Well shit.

"If you stay here, you're too far away for me to protect you." He held up his hand when she opened her mouth to protest. "Even if it's not warranted, I must have that peace of mind."

Fuck. Even if her father was a normal, regular dad, how could she argue with that?

"You're not going to let me see him again, are you?"

He shook his head again. Only once.

"Can I call him to say good-bye?"

Another head shake.

"Please. I don't want him to think I left and didn't want to talk to him."

"He's promised me he wouldn't contact you again."

Her mouth fell open. "You saw him? You talked to him?"

"Before coming here."

She narrowed her eyes. "You threatened him."

"I didn't have to. He offered that to me knowing it's the best thing for you." She glared at him, but she knew it was no more threatening than a water gun. "As angry at him as I am for not telling me about your midnight walks, and for keeping you out all night, I know he is a good man."

"So what would it hurt to call and say good-bye?"

"Why would you want to upset him, and yourself?"

"I don't," she whispered.

"Then leave it." He put his big, warm hand over her knee. "He knows, Sofia. Believe me, he knows." He stood and left the room.

In between the bouts of sobbing, she copied Matt's phone number into her bras and underwear before washing the number off *her arm. She cried the hardest when she did that. Now she wouldn't have anything of him to take home with her.*

Three hours later, she was sitting in her father's jet waiting to take off. To head home. To resume a life she'd put behind her.

After they were in the air, she went into the plane's little bedroom and slept fitfully. When she couldn't stand the tossing and turning anymore, she tried to piece together the cryptic things Matt had said to her last night – which felt like a hundred nights ago – and match them to the tiny bit of information her father had given her. She had no idea what was going on, but she came to the conclusion that the manners and the accent were for real, but the vibe was an act.

Matteo Parisi had weight on his soul he might never get rid of.

Lunchroom
Our Lady
Dutchford
Sofia

Amy looked like something the cat dragged in. She wasn't wearing anything resembling any of the variations of the school uniform. She had on super faded jeans, a thick black turtleneck sweater under her navy pea coat, and a huge pumpkin orange woolen scarf wrapped around her neck like ten times. Her hair was piled on top of her head in a messy topknot, and she wore hideous green fingerless gloves. She hadn't come to school in the morning, but she hauled her ass in a few minutes before lunch for Sofia. Matt's letter had arrived. And now Sofia knew. He didn't want her. All this time he'd been humoring her, biding his time until he told her, through a tour of Canada, to live her life without him.

After reading it three times to make certain there wasn't something she'd missed between the lines, she put her head down on her crossed arms, the stench of lunchroom cleaner infiltrating her nose, which rested millimeters away from the disgusting tabletop. She didn't bother to lift her head when she pushed the travel missive to Amy.

"Well, shit." Amy coughed.

Sofia lifted her head enough to turn it and lay her temple on her elbow. "You need to go home."

"Yeah, I do, but Monica told me to stay for the afternoon to get my assignments for the next few days and find out what I have to do to get caught up on what I missed."

"Do you feel the love from mommy dearest?"

"Every fuckin' day."

"Have you gone to the doctor?"

She nodded. "Bronchitis, with a side of sinus infection. I'm on horse antibiotics."

"I'm sorry, Ames. Can you sleep?"

"Only if I'm propped up on like six pillows, and only for a couple of hours at a time." Cough. Cough. Cough.

"You need a couple of shots of whiskey to loosen up your lungs and knock you out."

"Liquor's locked up since the last party."

Sofia nodded, her head movement sliding her crimson sweater up and down her wrist. "Almost worth it. Righteous party."

Amy grinned. "It was, wasn't it?" She pushed the letter back to Sofia. "So, whattaya going to do about that?"

Sofia shrugged. "What can I do? I mean, thinking back, he'd agreed to write the letters knowing all along he was going to use them to push me away." She sighed then sort of chuckled. "Ya know, this is so like him. He didn't want to break his word to my father, but he didn't want to upset me on the phone. He agreed to do this to be nice, and figured this was a gentle way to tell me there is no us."

"Good guy, though a fucked-up result." Cough.

"Yeah. He so is. And true. Sucks."

"Hairy monkey balls. But it gives you a chance to focus on you." Cough. "I mean, you've always known what you wanted to do. So do it."

"Hm. Heard from BU?"

"Yep. Northeastern too. Got into both."

"Knew you would."

"My cheerleader."

"Where are you going?"

"BU. It's got the Core curriculum, and it's a five-mile subway ride to Tufts."

Sofia had to smile. Amy. The bestest friend a girl could have. "I haven't heard from them yet."

"You will, and you'll get in. Your art is the shit."

"*My* cheerleader."

Amy laughed, then coughed. A lot. "I'm gonna crack a rib if I keep up this hacking."

"Don't talk."

"One last thing. How you gonna handle this? Crying jag, moping, alcohol, or stiff upper lip?"

"I'll mope in school. After I've sneaked a bottle of wine, I'll cry in my room, but I have to do stiff upper lip in front of the 'rents and *Nonna*. She can sniff out tears like a coonhound."

"Four months, Soph."

"I know. But right now turning eighteen with an entire summer yawning in front of me, I'm not feeling all 'I am Woman.'"

"Let's go to Canada."

Sofia actually laughed. Then thought about it. She watched Amy take her pills, drink down a bottle of water, drop her backpack on her chair, leave, probably to pee, come back, and look at her phone. A moment later the bell went off. "You know," she stood, grabbed the letter, folded it and stuffed it into her backpack, "you're right. Let's go to Canada."

Amy smiled and turned her phone so Sofia could see the search Amy had begun for airline tickets. Boston to Montreal, departing June 18th, two days after graduation, one day after Sofia's birthday.

"*Parle français* much?" Sofia asked.

Amy grinned.

Sofia walked Amy to the office where she had to turn in her "I was and am ill" note and meet with her guidance counselor, who would organize the arduous task of gathering Amy's schoolwork. God forbid a student wandered the halls and got her own homework. Our Lady had rules for their rules.

"Meet you at your locker after last bell."

Sofia nodded and went to the west stairwell shaking her head. She was headed to French class. Now, she'd actually have a chance to use what she'd learned.

Two and a half hours later, Amy and Sofia were leaning against the lockers waiting until the last possible moment before they had to go outside and leave. Amy's phone pinged.

"Shit."

"Monica?"

"Yeah. She's not good at waiting. Gotta book."

"'Kay. Hope I see you tomorrow."

"Chin up."

"No other choice."

Amy walked down the hall to the school's main doors.

Sofia lingered for a few more minutes, then headed out, and not a moment too soon. Tommie was standing next to the SUV, looking like he was about to come in and find her.

Plastering a neutral look on her face – she learned from the best, her father – she walked to the SUV chanting "Four months" in her head, but greeted Tommie with the manners of a perfect young lady. Gag.

Usually, especially on Tuesdays, when she was alone because Ro had choir practice, Sofia's mind wandered when she was in the back of the blacked-out monstrosity. Unlike Gio, who felt comfortable talking to anyone, or Ro, who interrogated everyone, Sofia didn't chat with Tommie or any of her father's men. They were solicitous, and probably could make small talk about things that weren't sports-related, but she had always felt like they were being nice because they had to be. They were paid to protect the family, not buddy up to them. Her father wouldn't've allowed his men to get familiar with his family, especially his kids, but he expected the men to be present and available while disappearing into the shadows at the same time.

Tommie had been with the family for fifteen years. Sofia couldn't remember a time when he wasn't around. She had no idea if he was married, had kids, or where he lived when he wasn't with them. She knew he loved dogs. Their Dobies, Sarah and Clyde, followed Tommie when he walked the perimeter. She'd seen him playing catch with them in the snow. That was the sum total of personal information she had about him.

He, on the other hand, knew all about the family. How could he not after watching over them at home and out in the world – he'd gone to Colorado with Gio last summer when he was there with Nat – for all these years. So, when he asked her, "What's wrong?" she wouldn't fallen off the wide bench seat if she didn't have her safety belt buckled.

She met his gaze in the rearview mirror. "Nothing." She shook her head.

"Try again."

She'd tell the truth as a lie. "Amy is sick. She was out last week and came in this afternoon to pick up her assignments. She might not be back for a couple of days."

He grunted. "What's she got?"

"Bronchitis and a sinus infection. She coughs all the time and is having a hard time sleeping."

"Rough."

"Yeah. She looked and sounded terrible."

He nodded.

That seemed to be the end of his concern. Thank Christ. She didn't want his attention or perception trained on her. The Amy story was real. He knew they were besties, and if Amy were ill, Sofia would be concerned. She decided a distraction was the way to go, something to keep her looking busy so she wouldn't have to engage with him anymore. She pulled her backpack over and put it on her lap. Before she got it open, he called out, "What's really wrong?"

Oh for fuck's sake. Her father must've ordered Tommie to keep a "special" eye on her. God, she hoped he didn't know what happened in Sicily.

"Nothing." He turned for a quick moment and she saw his scowl. "Really. I'm waiting to hear if I got into Tufts. That's it."

He didn't say anything, but she knew he didn't believe her. She'd say nothing to dissuade him. She knew he'd repeat their conversation verbatim to her father, and she sure as hell wasn't going to give him anything for her father to chew on.

"No one bothering you at school?"

She blinked a few times. Where did that come from? Ah, she was late coming out of the building. Anything off routine made Tommie suspicious. "At Our Lady?"

"Yeah."

She wanted to laugh. Everyone knew who her father was. There wasn't a mean girl alive who didn't have a honed sense of self-preservation. No one would say boo to Sofia, or shun her. Some girls might avoid her, but they were in the minority. She was invited to all the parties, was frequently surrounded by people at lunch, and was asked to sit on committees about dances with their "brother" school, Our Father. At least once a day someone told her they liked her hairstyle – it never changed – or asked if she saw *Riverdale*, *The Bachelorette*, or some other show, and what did she think? She knew they were all fake, but they were harmless. Whatever they said behind her back, they did it outside of school. She cared as much about them as they did about her.

"Not a single person."

He grunted again.

She opened her backpack and pulled out her French book. Of all things, today they'd partnered up and practiced ordering in restaurants. The timing couldn't've been better. She laid her backpack on the seat next to her, opened the book on her lap, and was flipping through the pages when the SUV swerved. Tommie cursed and righted the vehicle.

"You okay back there?"

"Yep." She looked at her backpack and saw its contents were on the seat and the floor. Shit. She didn't see Matt's letter.

"*Stunad* cut over from the left turn lane."

"I'm fine. No worries." She saw they were turning into her driveway and she unbuckled her seatbelt to gather up her stuff. When the car stopped at the gate, she got down on the floor and looked beneath the seat for Matt's letter. She didn't see it anywhere.

She rechecked her backpack and the seat. The car moved up the drive to the house and stopped. She ran her hand between the entire seam between the seat back and the bench. Nothing. Back to the floor, where she was patting underneath the seats feeling for the envelope. A shaft of light came through the back when Tommie opened the door.

"Waddya doing?"

"Gathering up the stuff that flew out of my backpack when we swerved," she told the underside of the bench.

"Get outta there and lemme look."

Oh hell to the no. "Give me a sec, okay. I know what I'm looking for."

"Soph, there ain't nothing in this car except what flew outta ya bag. Whatever I find, it's yours."

Damn straight it was, and he wasn't getting his mitts anywhere near her stuff. "One more minute."

She straightened up but was still on her knees when Tommie reached into the side pocket of the door and held up the envelope with Matt's letter in it. "This what you looking for?"

Take a deep breath. Appear calm. "Yep." She held out her hand.

He turned over the envelope and read it. "This don't look like school stuff. And it's addressed to Amy."

She wiggled her fingers. "It's mine."

"This what upset ya?"

Jesus, Mary, and Joseph. All the saints and the apostles. Someone. Anyone. Give her a hand here. "Nope." She walked on her knees to the open door, then wiggled her fingers again. "I'll take that now."

"Soph, you're crawling around the car on your hands and knees freakin' out looking for this thing. I'm thinking it's sumpin' that upset ya."

Lord, hear my prayer. "It's mine, Tommie. I'd like it back now."

"Ya know," he tilted his head toward his enormous shoulder, "I'm thinkin' it's sumpin' the Don should take a look at."

"He respects my privacy." That right there was a huge, ginormo lie. "He doesn't read my mail."

"Well, this ain't addressed to ya, so no worries." He stuffed the envelope with Matt's letter inside – MATT'S LETTER – into his inside jacket pocket.

Damage control. That was Sofia's first and only thought. She left her backpack and stumbled out of the car, flying past Tommie, and ran into the house. *Nonna* called out to her, but Sofia kept running, moving down one hall, then another, rounding the corner to commit the most giant no-no – much worse than any sin – in their household. She didn't knock, she didn't wait for her father to say, "Come in." She pushed through his study's door, which was no easy feat cuz that sucker weighed a ton, swung the door behind her, hoping it closed, and took in her father's face as he stood from his huge executive chair and leaned his large hands on his desk, his eyes blue molten fire.

"Don't yell," she shouted. He looked like he was going to combust. His usually placid, olive-toned face was mottled with red blotches that seemed to go all the way down his neck. "Listen to me before you say or do anything." His hands balled into fists but remained on his desk. "You have to hear me out."

"Leave it here, Tommie, and close the door on your way out."

Out of the corner of her eye, she saw Tommie walking to her father's desk, where he dropped the envelope with Matt's letter in it on the corner of the desk closest to her father's left hand. Tommie turned, walked away, and she heard the door snick closed. Until that moment she didn't realize she was standing two feet in front of the desk, trembling so hard her skirt shook against her knees.

"I'm waiting," her father ground out as if the words had to force themselves past his clenched teeth.

"I love you, but you're suffocating the hell out of me. It's like I'm living in the Dark Ages. You took away my car and my cell. No one's allowed to call the house, and you won't let me call anyone from the house except Gio. Since I've been back, I can't go to any parties, dances, or even Amy's house. The only time I've been *anywhere* is when you let me go with Gio and Nat to those Halloween parties. I'm guessing you had someone tailing us, but I never saw them, so I had a good time."

"Was that good time before or after you called Matteo?" His voice rumbled through the room, and she swore she saw the papers flutter on his desk.

You see, this was what'd slipped her mind. Since she'd been back home her life had been an endless cycle of whooshing dips and then chugging up a hill like a roller coaster, but without any of the fun. In her emotional upheaval, she'd forgotten about her father's reach. She'd forgotten he knew everything. About everyone. All the fucking time. How? She had no idea.

She had been careful. Deliberate. No one, absolutely no one knew anything but Amy. Sofia had used Amy's phone in the bathroom in a house of some college guys she didn't even know. She hadn't talked to Matt for more than a few minutes. The text he sent back with his correspondent's number went to Amy's phone. The letters went through TLC to Amy's house. Amy gave Sofia Matt's letters. Sofia gave her replies to Amy to mail. It was contained. Only Amy knew. Only Amy.

Amy.

"Amy?"

He tilted his head slightly to the right.

Holy fuck. Sofia had been betrayed by the only true friend she had on earth.

She crumpled to the ground.

The Study
Di Caro residence
Dutchford
Sofia

She didn't stay down for more than a moment. Her father appeared at her side and lifted her into his big, strong arms, then carried her to the sofa in front of the fireplace where he sat, and not since she was a little girl, he placed her on his lap and lightly pressed her head against his wide, solid chest.

"Forgive her," he murmured in her ear. "I can be persuasive."

Well, there was an understatement if she ever heard one.

Sitting there, being *contained*, she wanted to scream at the top of her lungs. She wanted to punch him in the face. She wanted to sob her eyes out. Instead, she waited and she listened.

"Remember," his deep voice was barely above a whisper, "when I told you there were things you didn't know and never would?"

She nodded against his chest. He was talking about Matt's family.

"I've been protecting you from those things."

She jolted and fisted his crisp tailored shirt.

"No car means you're not alone on the road. No phone means no one can track you or hack you. No parties mean no one can put anything in your drink. No visiting Amy means she's not in danger if someone comes for you."

There was so much there, and so much he wasn't saying, it made what he was saying somehow scarier. By now, the trembling was back with a vengeance, making her fingers curl and tighten in his shirt.

"I don't want you scared, my precious Sofia, I want you safe so you can live your life to its fullest, and for a very, very long time. Until this danger passes, I'm asking you to trust me to keep you and the rest of my family safe."

"Wh…what about Gio an…and Nat. Th…they're, they're –"

"Protected at all times. People are there watching out for them."

"Do…do they know?"

"That they're protected?"

She nodded.

"Absolutely."

She wondered how Nat handled that. Gio was born to this life. Nat was marrying into it.

Always adept at reading people, her father answered her unasked question. "Natalia is a practical woman. She understands who her future husband is and accepts all of the realities that come with him."

Damn. How did he do that? Say everything without saying anything.

He tightened his arms for moment. "Are you up for answering some questions?"

She nodded.

"What do you want?"

She loosened the hold on his shirt but didn't let go when she leaned back to look up at him. "For…for real?"

His lips twitched. "For real."

Deep breath, get it out all in one go. "Is Matt pushing me away because of you?"

He didn't keep her waiting. "In part. Mostly, he wants you safe."

Her head swam and the clench around her heart loosened. "If," she wasn't practiced at speaking in code, but she tried, "he didn't have to…worry about keeping me safe, do you think…"

"No." Her heart dropped to her knees. "I know."

Elation. "Is there a way for him to…not worry about keeping me safe?"

"There is."

"Then I want him."

"For real?"

She yanked on her father's shirt and tried to smile up at him. "Absolutely."

"You're sure?"

"I know you think I'm too young to make such a monumental decision about the rest of my life, but Gio was only three years older than me when he fell in love with Nat *through the mail*."

"Those are three big years, my Sofia."

"I get that." She couldn't argue facts. "How'd you know with Mom?"

Again, he answered with no hesitation. "I couldn't imagine living my life without her."

Wow. She was shocked he didn't tell her he was older, had more experience, they took their time, yada, yada. "Must run in the family."

She heard the soft chuckle in his chest. "So it seems. What about university?"

"None of that changes. For as long as I can remember, I've wanted to study and learn all I could about my art so I could devote my life to it. Matt knows this, and he wants it for me. He'd never stand in my way."

"I'd have to agree."

"You know, I'm smart and determined."

He gave me a small smile. "I'm well aware."

"I'm not fragile."

"I never thought you were."

"You treat me like I'll break if a strong wind blows near me."

"I treat your mother, sister, grandmother, and now Natalia the same way."

"But not Gio."

"No. The feeling is the same, but I am a product of my upbringing. He's my son."

"So old school."

"I'm all right with that."

She slapped his chest lightly. "Why haven't we done this before? Not the crisis stuff. The talking."

"A mistake I intend to rectify."

"At the beginning of the summer, before you left Sicily, when you took me to lunch?"

He nodded. Once.

"One of the best times I've ever had with you."

"Then we'll do it more often."

She didn't want to move back to the heavy, but she had to know. "What now?"

He understood what she was asking. Sometimes, she thought he read minds. "You have to trust me to protect you even if it means you live in the 'Dark Ages' a while longer. Can you do that?"

She nodded.

"No more letters, Sofia. You must promise me."

"I promise."

"No more phone calls either."

"I won't call him, Dad."

"Good." He gave her a squeeze. "When I'm comfortable your safety is no longer compromised, you'll know, and so will Matteo."

She wrapped her arms around him, well, as far as they would go and spoke into his chest. "The waiting is going to be rough."

"You can handle it."

"I have no choice."

"In this, no, you don't."

"It sucks."

He lifted her chin with his forefinger and gave her his half grin. "I'm sure it does."

"I have a request."

He tilted his chin down.

"Talk to us more at the dinner table."

His eyes widened enough to for her to know, she'd surprised him.

He gave her a full smile this time. "I'll give it a try."

"I love you, Dad."

"The best words a father ever hears."

The Lunchroom
Our Lady
Two Days Later
Sofia

Sofia knew Amy had come back to school today and was avoiding her. Her father must've told Amy the cat was out of the bag, and, knowing Amy, she didn't want to get into it with Sofia. And who could blame her. Really, nobody ever said no to Don Alessandro. While Sofia had no idea who the people were with whom her father did business, she had been around him at every family function for nearly eighteen years, and she remembered about fourteen of those years.

Outside their immediate family gatherings, there wasn't a dinner, christening, confirmation, bar/bat mitzvah, wedding, funeral, holiday party, or celebration that had fewer than forty people in attendance. Typically, there were about three hundred people or more. And every single adult, from the *nonnos and nonna*s, the old *zia*s and *zio*s, to Mom and Dad's brothers, sisters, nephews and nieces, almost all of whom were successful in their own right – business owners, doctors, lawyers, executives – every one of them showed deference to Don Alessandro. Sought out his advice on a wide range of subjects, many times disappearing for an hour, cloistered in the Don's study while the party carried on. Aside from Uncle Aaron, who had defied his brother-in-law long before they'd become in-laws, which was probably why Dad still held a mean grudge, Sofia couldn't think of a relative who didn't mentally genuflect when asking for the Don's ear.

Amy was feisty and had a mouth on her, but facing the pressure the Don must've applied to get Amy to rat on Sofia? Amy caved. Maybe not at first, or all at once, but she never had a snowball's chance in hell of saying no to him.

Sofia sat in the middle of the lunchroom, conspicuously alone, letting Amy know Sofia wasn't hiding. That she'd welcome an approach. But the proverbial ball was in Amy's court, so all Sofia could do was wait. After about ten minutes of looking busy skimming her World Studies outline, Sofia heard the rustling of what sounded like a plastic bag behind her. She'd bet Sriracha Sunshine Hippeas. Sure enough, a bright yellow bag was dropped in front of her before Amy rounded the table.

"Peace offering?" Sofia looked at the snack.

"If it'll work." Amy tilted her head and stuck out her bottom lip in an exaggerated pout.

"Anyone else, I'd be pissed. But c'mon. Who says no to him?"

"Right?" Amy breathed out a long sigh. "I mean, I tried to say no. Really."

"I believe you."

"But day-um. He knows how to play that guilt violin like a concert master."

"He's had a lot of practice."

"It shows." Amy wiped her brow. "I was shitting bricks and shaking in my boots at the same time."

Sofia couldn't help it, she laughed.

Amy looked relieved. "All he told me was, you knew, and he figured we'd talk."

"We've come to an understanding."

Amy made a rolling motion with her hand. "And?"

"Everything he'd doing is to keep me safe from some danger he refuses to tell me about."

"Hmm."

"Honestly? I don't want to know. It's not that I think I couldn't handle it, but it'll be another thing swirling around in my head, and I've got enough unwanted shit piled in there to last me two lifetimes."

"Amen to that, sister."

"So, on the one hand, I *realllly* don't like him treating me as if I'd get the vapors from too much info, on the other, I'm okay with not knowing. I trust that it's fairly awful when he says there's danger he's protecting me from."

"He doesn't strike me as someone who does drama."

Sofia barked out a laugh. "He's the last person on earth who'd create drama. He's all about control."

"Oh yeah. I saw that up close and in person." Amy fanned her face.

"Since he and I talked, I've been thinking of all the fucked-up things that happen to ordinary people just living their lives. Then I layered on being his kid. His daughter no less – he's so old school – and up until my asshole ex went all gonzo, I wasn't hemmed in. I knew he kept a close watch, but he never said I couldn't do anything. I figure, if he's worried enough to go all Dark Ages on me, I need to respect that."

"Look at you being all reasonable and adult." Amy grabbed the bag of Hippeas and pulled the sides and the top seam separated. She tilted the bag to Sofia and she took a few.

"Something he said made me settle."

More hand motions from Amy, whose mouth was stuffed.

"He told me Matt was pushing me away partly because of him, but mostly because he wanted me safe. Then he was vague, but what I took away from it was once Matt knew the danger was gone, we would be free to be…" she shrugged, "us."

"And in the meantime?" Amy sucked each fingertip.

"No more letters. No more phone calls."

"Harsh."

Sofia nodded. "Don't have much choice."

"Too true." Amy tilted her head. "You know I'm not all Pollyanna and shit like that, but I think everything's going to be all right, Soph. I'm not blowing smoke or anything. I really feel it's all going to work out."

Sofia sighed. "From your mouth, Ames."

Vittoria, Sicily
Matteo

After church, Enzo approached Matteo and said, "Let's walk."

Matteo turned to tell his father to wait, but the old man, who'd aged fifty years since his sons had died, had taken in the situation and waved at Matteo to go with Enzo. Dad was chatting with the priest and a few neighbors, and would probably be in that exact spot when Matteo got back after hearing whatever Enzo had to say.

With the exception of the Di Caro family coming to Vittoria, Matteo's family had little to do with the Contis. From what Matteo's father had told him, the Parisis and the Contis were cordial, but they didn't socialize. No bad blood, simply a matter of different business interests and alliances.

The moment Enzo had moved into the center aisle after mass and headed in Matteo's direction, he knew Enzo was delivering a message from the Don. When Don Alessandro had come to the Parisi family home after Matteo had kept Sofia out all night, the Don had told him any further communications would go through Enzo.

That was the easiest part of a conversation Matteo would have given his left nut not to've had.

After Matteo had seen Sofia slip into the back door of the house, he'd walked the kilometre to his car, got in and sat, staring out the windshield at the lightening sky. Everything about the previous seven hours had been glorious and tragic. He'd never believed soul mates existed. To've found his in a seventeen-year-old girl had been a cruel twist of fate, and it felt as if the cosmos were laughing at him. There were so many "ifs" attached to him and Sofia, neither Sophocles nor Shakespeare could've conjured a play with more heartbreak attached to it.

As he started the ignition, Matteo wished he could be *that guy*. The one who fucked his sorrow away. But he wasn't built like that. While he'd had his share of lovers, they'd all meant something, even if their liaisons had been brief. If he were the type of man who could bury his cock in a random as a means to obliterate his heartache, it wouldn't change his underlying reality: he'd never find another Sofia.

Nothing for it, he'd put his car in gear and drove home.

Going to bed would have been folly. He would have lain there, staring at the ceiling for hours. Instead, he'd gone into the kitchen, had a quick conversation with Lina, their housekeeper, who left the room to get on with her morning routine. Matteo made coffee and put out the fresh *cornetto* on a large round plate. By the time his father came into the kitchen, fully dressed in his dark grey suit and solid dark blue silk tie set against a crisp white shirt, Matteo was leaning against the large marble-topped center island reading the newspaper, his cappuccino steaming from the cup next to his elbow.

"*Ciao, Papa. Espresso o cappuccino?*"

"*Cappuccino, figliolo.*" Matteo nodded at his dad, wondering if calling him son dug a knife into his father's heart as much as it hurt Matteo to hear it. He was his father's only living child now, and knowing what Matteo had to do, that designation might not be true in a couple of months. "*Vado in citta' per oggi. Forse ceneremo più tardi.*"

"Sure, Papa," Matteo told his father in Italian. "Do you want to have dinner here or in town?"

"*Ti chiamo più tardi e ti faccio sapere.*" His father took his *cappuccino* and put a *cornetto* on a small plate, and then stood across the island from Matteo, who'd pushed the sports section to his father.

"Okay. I'll wait for your call."

At nine on the dot, his father exited through the kitchen door, crossed the long tiled patio, his gait no longer spry, and climbed into the backseat of his waiting car, his driver, Vito, shutting the door after a much aged-looking Edoardo Parisi.

Matteo finished his coffee and walked up the back staircase to his rooms. Lina had thrown open the curtains and all the doors to the balcony, letting in a breeze that portended colder weather. He'd felt the chill settle in him last night and figured, regardless of the weather, he'd never truly be warm again.

When Lina came in to tell him he had a visitor, Matteo had been working at his desk. He checked his phone, saw it was three in the afternoon, and said to himself, *right on time*. The morning had come and gone, and Enzo hadn't come by to beat the shit of out him, which meant that honour would be reserved for Don Alessandro, who, as sure as the sun rose in the east, would not let Matteo's behaviour stand, and would fly across the Atlantic to take that message to him personally.

The Don was in the library where Lina had left him, standing in the middle of the room, his gaze trained on the doorway. Everything Matteo had heard about the man was true, and then some. Tall, a powerful trim build, classically handsome, a light dusting of silver threaded through his black hair at his temples and around his crown. He wore a bespoke suit and did not look like he'd made a ten-hour trip from Boston to Vittoria. He appeared calm and collected. But Matteo understood the illusion for what it was. He felt the man's restrained power bouncing off the walls of the vast library.

Matteo walked right up to the Don, stuck out his hand, and said, "On my honour, nothing happened last night, and I swear, such an evening will not be repeated. I promise you, I will not contact her again."

Up close, Matteo could see the Don's bright blue eyes blazed like a flame, his scrutiny sharp and thorough as he assessed the veracity of Matteo's statement. After what seemed like two days, the Don grasped Matteo's hand and held on tight when he said, "You understand I take promises seriously."

Matteo would've gulped if there were any saliva left in his mouth. "I do, sir."

The Don nodded once, released Matteo's hand then walked right by him. Between exhaustion and the vacuum the Don's forceful exit created, Matteo could have sworn he swayed. He heard the Don's heavy footfall on the marble-tiled floor before the front door closed a minute later.

Now, walking alongside Enzo, Matteo tried to prepare himself for the Don's message, which he was certain was not going to be good. He presumed the Don had learned Matteo had broken his promise, and it didn't surprise him Sofia and Matteo's letters had been discovered. Matteo almost chuckled thinking about how careful Sofia believed she'd been. Surely, after her father had "rescued" her from Sicily following her having spent an entire night with a twenty-two-year-old man, the Don would go beyond his usual diligence to make beyond certain he was fully apprised of Sofia's every move.

Matteo and Enzo walked down the hill to the bottom of the parking lot, where Enzo stopped and turned slowly in a circle, scanning the lot and the trees beyond before placing himself in front of Matteo. Enzo leaned in, and in a raspy whisper said, "One week from this Wednesday, be at a place with good security somewhere in Germany or the Netherlands. Next Sunday, after mass, you'll tell me where."

Matteo nodded, Enzo stepped back, and they made their way back through the parking lot to the bottom of the church steps, where Edoardo Parisi was talking to his neighbors and the priest, exactly where Matteo had left him.

***

The next day, Matteo made the arrangements, which was the easiest thing he'd tackled in the past twenty-four hours. The evening before his father had gone off the rails, unfortunately an increasingly common occurrence. There was nothing Matteo could say to relieve his father's unrelenting self-recriminations. For hours, he'd listened to his dad alternately yell and sob over the loss of his sons. In between the bouts of anger and grief, Matteo was re-reminded of his duties to his family. As if he needed his memory jogged since that had been, singularly, the constant topic of discussion from the moment Matteo had returned to Sicily. His father was past impatient, believing swift and violent retribution was the only solution while Matteo had other ideas, and was slow to execute them in the hopes he could talk his father off his vengeance ledge.

As expected, after Due and Mariano had been killed, Dad had been inconsolable. Matteo had gotten the news early the morning after their deaths had been discovered. He'd been in his flat sleeping off one of his last nights of carousing with his mates before he was scheduled to start working in his new position – his dream job – the following Monday.

Between his third and fourth year at Cambridge, he'd had an internship with a high-profile London finance firm that specialized in funding sustainable and renewable energy companies worldwide. They'd thought well of his work and offered him a position after graduation. He'd been scheduled to start the third week in June and had been enjoying a few weeks of freedom when his father had called with the devastating news.

Half drunk, he'd called the managing partner at the firm and explained why he couldn't take the job. To his great relief and surprise, he was told they'd hold the position for him when he returned from his bereavement. Unbelievably, every month when he called to say he needed more time, he was told his job would be waiting for him when he returned. While his best mate from Eton and Cambridge, whose grandfather had been the founding partner of the firm, denied being Matteo's champion, he knew better.

Nearly nine months had passed since he'd learned his was an only child, and he was no closer to returning to London and his old life than a dodo had a chance of flying. Matteo felt much like that unfortunate extinct bird. He'd been the one who got away. A Parisi not chained to his familial history. A man who'd adapted to his new environment and had thrived, only to be pulled back and tasked to become the person he was never meant to be, and who he despised: the avenging angel of his brothers' murders.

In general, Matteo had always known about his family's "business," but he'd left Sicily at the age when he would've begun being in schooled in what that "business" entailed. Only when he had been sitting next to his father in the family's private plane on the tarmac of a private airfield in Berkshire, England, had Matteo learned he was being sent to Eton *for his own good*, was to remain in England to continue his studies, and stay in England when he began a career befitting his education. Briefly, but with absolute conviction, his father had informed him his life was to take a different path than the rest of the Parisis. After a hug and kisses on both cheeks, thirteen-year-old Matteo had de-planed alone, gotten into a waiting limousine, and was taken to Eton College.

Now, as far removed from the life his father and brothers had lived, Matteo had to do the unthinkable: annihilate the La Rosa family for killing Due and Mariano.

***

One Year Ago

Due couldn't believe this shit. Thirty-three years old and he was still dragging his thirty-one-year-old brother's ass out from between a woman's legs. But this time when Due lifted Mariano off his bed, Due cursed and smacked his brother across the face, then threw the covers over the naked girl tangled in his brother's sheets.

"What the fuck were you thinking?"

Mariano stirred, leaning his naked body against his brother and slurred, "That that was my pussy."

Goddamn it. This time Mariano had fucked the wrong girl. Nineteen-year-old Adriana La Rosa was a notorious wildcat. The girl raised more hell than all five of her brothers combined. The baby of the family had been too babied and hadn't grown out of being a willful brat. It didn't help that she looked like a young Gina Lollobrigida with her long dark hair and a body that defined the word sin.

"Her old man and all five of her brothers are going to kill you slowly if you don't marry her."

Mariano shrugged. "I wanna marry her. She's pregnant with my kid."

Due pushed his brother into a chair and threw his jeans at him. "So what's the fucking problem?"

"She doesn't wanna get married." He tried three times to get his leg into the jeans, gave up, and slouched back in the chair. "Says I won't make a good husband. I'll run around on her and shit like that."

Apparently, Adriana was smarter than Due gave her credit for. "Take a shower. Drink coffee. Then wake her up. I don't care what the fuck you have to do, but by five o'clock this afternoon she better be wearing your engagement ring. I'll go with you when you take her home to her father and ask his permission to marry her."

Mariano shook his head. "Man, I'm telling you, she won't do it." He stood on wobbly legs and half stumbled to the nightstand where he took a blue velvet box out of the drawer and then threw it to Due. "Got the ring two months ago and I've been trying to give it to her practically every night since."

Due opened the box and saw a big-ass diamond surrounded by rubies. "No more trying. Today you're going to do it."

Mariano made it back to the chair and collapsed. "Don't Yoda my ass."

"I'm going to beat your ass if this shit isn't settled by the time I get back this afternoon."

Due left to take care of business his brother was to supposed to do along with him. When Due returned, he found Mariano at his desk working on his laptop. "So?"

"So she left before I got out the shower. She won't answer my calls or texts. I have no idea where the fuck she is."

Due ran his fingers through his hair. "Did you look for her?"

"Man, she's been playing this game with me for five fuckin' months. She could be anywhere. Malta for all I know." He got up and paced behind his desk. "Into her. Love her. She doesn't believe me. I don't mind working for it, but I'm done chasing her. She'll show up when she shows up. We'll fight. We'll fuck, and she'll stay for a while, then she'll get a wild hair and take off."

"Where does her father think she is?"

"In college. Studying."

"Is she?"

"When the spirit moves her."

"Enough. You got to nail this shit down, brother. C'mon. Bring the ring."

Three hours later they found her sitting alone poolside at a girlfriend's house, an iPad propped on bended knees. Due stood in front of the door leading into the house and watched his brother move across the deck. He stood staring at his girl before he sat on the edge of her longue. He took the iPad and put it on the ground before he leaned in and pressed his hand against her belly. Whatever he said, and he talked a while, made her dip her chin then nod. He took out the ring and slid it on finger. She scooted down and kissed him like she hadn't seen him in months. Smiling, he wrapped his arm around her waist and helped her up. She grabbed her bag from the table beside the longue, bent to get the iPad, pushed it into the bag, then slung it over her shoulder.

Mariano took her hand, and they walked to Due.

An hour later Due was sitting across from Adriana at the kitchen table in her father's house sipping espresso waiting for Mariano to come back from talking with her father in his study.

When Mariano finally walked in, he had a wad of tissues pressed against his bleeding bottom lip. He held out the tissues. "Don La

Rosa wasn't happy the wedding has to happen within the next two weeks."

Adriana groaned. "You can't be surprised."

"Not complaining, bella."

She smiled, and he bent down and kissed the tip of her nose.

Two weeks and two days later, they had a huge church wedding, festooned with flowers, bows, bridesmaids and groomsmen, as if the spectacle had been planned for months. An ostentatious reception was held on the grounds of Don La Rosa's home and was attended by over two hundred people.

Three months later, Adriana, six months pregnant, was heading home to her and Mariano's house in the hills above Vittoria after she'd had dinner with a couple of girlfriends. When she drove past a hotel in town and saw Mariano kissing a woman on the cheek in front of his car, Adriana, being Adriana, pulled up alongside the car and yelled, "I knew it. You bastard. You promised." She sped off, and Mariano followed. The woman whom he'd been kissing good-bye on the cheek was one of the Parisi's attorneys.

Adriana had driven erratically for eight kilometres when she made a sharp turn onto a narrow road going up a hill leading out of town. Mariano watched as his wife's car went off the road. He jumped out of his car and saw his wife's vehicle roll into a ravine, coming to a stop after it slammed into an old olive tree.

Three days after burying his wife and unborn child, Mariano Parisi's dead body was left on the back patio of his house alongside the dead body of his brother, Due. Payment for the two lives Don La Rosa had lost, which he blamed on Mariano.

***

His father had told Matteo the story so many times, he felt like he'd been there. Each time, his father ended with a slew of rhetorical questions, most of which boiled down to, "Why?" Then the rants would start, voicing in lurid detail all the horrors Edoardo Parisi intended Matteo to rain down on the La Rosa family in retribution for the deaths of Due and Mariano. Matteo. A finance guy who went to Eton and Cambridge and had a job waiting for him at a prestigious London firm where he intended to help the earth by getting money to renewable and sustainable energy companies.

Maybe when he met with Don Alessandro next week, Matteo would lead with his alternative method of *annihilating* the La Rosa family. He prayed the request, and its implementation, would serve as a distraction and keep Matteo alive after breaking his promise.

It seemed the Parisi brothers couldn't help but fuck up royally when it came to whom they fell in love with and how they handled it.

Soho House
Berlin, Germany
Matteo

"Good afternoon, Don." Matteo motioned Don Alessandro into the suite and saw a large, menacing man take position in the hallway outside the suite's door.

The Don nodded his greeting. Matteo took the Don's coat and hung it in the front closet as Don Alessandro looked around the lushly appointed suite. "When did you become a member?"

Matteo went to the sideboard and poured two fingers of an exclusive small-batch whiskey into a tumbler, added two cubes of ice, then crossed to the large side chair beside which Don Alessandro stood straight and tall. After handing him the glass, Matteo replied, "I'm not. A mate from Cambridge is and arranged the suite for me."

Don Alessandro lowered himself into the chair, and Matteo went to the sofa and sat opposite him, watching as the long-limbed, elegant man crossed his legs at the knee, brushed the material, then took a sip of the whiskey. He gave Matteo a small grin, then rested his hand holding the tumbler on the arm of the chair.

Matteo summoned all the courage he had and dove in. "With your permission, I'd like to get right to it."

"But of course."

"I broke my promise to you, and I am sorry. Truly. I should have never made the promise in the first place, and I should have talked to you when I knew I wasn't able to keep it. I meant and mean no disrespect." The Don nodded once, which could signify *okay keep going*, or *I acknowledge you're shit on the bottom of my shoe, but I'll sit here and sip the expensive whiskey you know I drink and listen to you until I decide how to dispose of you.* "As you are aware," Matteo continued, "and this is an explanation, not an excuse. Intentionally, at his behest, and later because I continued to honour my father's wishes, I am not of his world and was never meant to be."

Again, the Don nodded once.

"I know what I'm supposed to do regarding my father's…business. The truth, and again, no disrespect, I don't want any part of it. Were I to…begin what is expected, there is no turning back. Undoubtedly, my brothers' deaths must be…dealt with. There is no argument there, but the manner in which the…matter would be handled is problematic." Matteo watched the Don's impassive face and thought, *fifty-fifty I'll be alive in an hour.* "I have an idea about how to handle the…situation. Instead of…in-kind retribution, perhaps dismantling their source of income would achieve…a palatable result. Doing this properly would require more than computer keystrokes. I'd need someone, or a consortium, to buy up the detritus of the businesses to keep the…offending family from rebuilding. I thought to ask your guidance and blessing on this course of action."

The Don tilted his head slightly to the left. Matteo waited in the heavy silence, not moving a muscle even though his insides were vibrating. "She's not yet eighteen."

Whoa. All right. Okay. We're back there. Shit. "On my mother's soul, I have never so much as kissed her."

"I know." That hung in the air for a long moment so Matteo could absorb what wasn't said, but implied: *It's why you're still breathing.* "And when she is of legal age?"

"She'll be at Tufts in their art museum program. She starts in the fall."

"That's what *she's* going to do. I'm asking about you."

"I want to be with her any way she'll have me." When he saw the Don's eyes start to narrow, Matteo hurried to say, "I mean as her boyfriend, or fiancé, or…husband." Matteo knew he should have been smoother about this, but fuck it. His life was on the line anyway. "I love her. I want to spend the rest of my life with her."

"I expect her to experience college fully."

"As do I."

"And London?"

"I can let the flat while she's at university. My firm… The firm that offered a position to me has an office in Boston."

"Financing and funding sustainable energy projects, is it?"

"Yes." As if Don Alessandro didn't know everything about Matteo, inside and out, upside down and backwards.

The Don put his unfinished glass of whiskey on the coffee table then stood. Matteo didn't know if he should bring up his idea about his brothers' retribution again, ask if the Don needed Matteo to explain some more of the plan, or what. *Shit.* Since he had no idea what would happen next, he waited and listened to his heart bang against his rib cage.

"Since you intend to be a member of *my* family, I'll speak to your father about taking care of his problem and his businesses." He stared at Matteo meaningfully. "All of the family businesses."

Fuck. Wow. Um, what did he say to that? In one fell swoop, Don Alessandro gave Matteo his blessing to marry Sofia, so much as said, "I'll handle avenging your brothers," and everything that went with it, and, without blinking, announced he intended to take over all of the Parisi family's considerable holdings, many of which were legit. *Payment for breaking the promise.*

Matteo stuck out his hand.

The Don looked down at it and time was suspended before he took it and shook, clasping his other hand over Matteo's. *Okay. That means good things, right?*

"Don't go back to Sicily. Leave here and return to London. Make arrangements with your firm to work out of London for the next three months then have them transfer you to their Boston office at the beginning of June." Matteo's knees almost gave out from the relief and the adrenaline crash. He managed to make it to the front closet and retrieve the Don's coat. When he handed it to him, Don Alessandro said in a deep tone that revealed a shimmer of his power, "*Never* break a promise to her."

Then he left.

Matteo leaned his back against the closed door and slid his arse to the floor.

Holy shit.

Theresa Calapiano's new office
Dutchford
Sofia

"Wow. I like it." Sofia turned in a circle in the reception area, taking in the eight turquoise office chairs, separated by a couple of small tables with magazines on them. On the opposite side of the room, check-in signs sat on a light wood curved desk, above which were two super-large photographs of the ocean with wide sand beaches and palm trees in the foreground. She walked through the door to the office and saw the theme repeated in a light turquoise sofa with tan pillows that had brown wavy stitching through them, and a carved light wood desk with a dark turquoise executive chair. Pearl white side chairs faced the desk, which matched the upholstered wing chair facing the couch. Large seashells and starfish were interspersed throughout the three offset light wood short shelving that topped what looked like a light wood credenza, but was probably file cabinets. She leaned against the desk and said, "It's bright and airy. The beach and sand colors are soothing."

"I thought so." Theresa smiled up from her perch at the end of the sofa. "I thought the ocean theme would have a calming effect."

"Must be a thing this year. My mother did up Christmas with beachy stuff."

Theresa smiled. "You've said she has good taste and is trendy, so no doubt, it's a thing this year."

Not for the first time, Sofia thought Theresa's compassion and empathy made her a great therapist, but Sofia's affinity for the woman was her size. Petite and small-boned like Sofia, but with thick dark hair and piercing golden brown eyes. At first glance, Theresa seemed delicate, but one look at that intense gaze, and all thoughts of fragile and dainty flew out the window.

"When do you officially open?"

"Next Monday."

"Are you nervous?" *Damn.* Sofia clapped her hand over her mouth, her eyes widening at the gaff.

Theresa laughed then stood. "It's all right. A perfectly reasonable question."

Sofia shook her head. "Matteo would say, 'Bad form.'"

"Maybe if we weren't close. But I think it's safe to say since we are, and in a way that forged a bond, I'd ask the same question if the shoe was on the other foot."

In a small voice, Sofia said, "I wish we didn't have that bond."

"Aw, Soph. I know you know you're not responsible for what he did. As time goes along and you see I'm fine, you'll feel it in here," she pointed to her chest, "as well as in here." She pointed to her head. "And to answer your question, I'm not nervous. I'm chomping at the bit to return to work. My therapist told me I'd know when I was ready, and she was right. I knew a few weeks ago, and as soon as I did, I scouted for office space then set about getting it organized."

"Okay. Then I'm happy for you."

"You hungry?"

"Starved."

"Greek?"

"You read my mind."

As they picked over the remains on the sampling platter, Sofia told the story of Tommie discovering the letter, and Sofia learning about how her father coerced Amy into being an informant.

"Did you forgive her?" Theresa asked as she pushed hummus onto a small piece of pita bread.

"Yeah. Like immediately. I mean, who says no to my father?"

Theresa nodded while chewing, swallowed and muttered, "Don't I know it."

"I *knew* he took care of everything while you recovered."

"He's…"

"Super grateful, and has been like ridiculously generous to show how grateful."

"That sums it up nicely."

"I love you're so polite. Listen, one of the things I came to terms with early on is that I'm not from a normal family." Sofia waved away the comment she saw Theresa forming. "I know, I know. There's no such thing as a normal family. And I realize I'm fortunate in many ways, but let's be real, my life has been different from day one. For the past seven months, I've been living in Middle Ages mode because some intense shit is going down with Matt's family and my father is involved. Until that's taken care of," she shook her head, "and I don't want to know what that even means, but I can guess, Matt and I are on ice."

"One bright spot," Theresa always found silver linings, "now you know there's potential for you and Matteo."

Sofia smiled. "Definitely a bright spot." She pointed to the last stuffed grape leaf. "You want that?"

Theresa shook her head. "You eat it."

Sofia bit into the goodness of herbed rice, olive oil, and lemon and let out a "yum" noise.

Theresa chuckled.

"For real," Sofia talked around licking her fingers, "I could eat those every day."

"So I see."

"Another bright spot," Sofia wiped her hands on her napkin, "I got into Tufts."

"Oh Soph, that's fantastic, and no small achievement."

"I gotta say, I'm pretty proud of myself."

"As well you should be."

"Will you come to my graduation party?"

"I wouldn't miss it for the world."

Sofia smiled. "If for no other reason to see I'm not lying about how nauseating Gio and Nat are."

Theresa laughed. "I'm looking forward to it."

"You say that now."

Bloomsbury Street
Matteo's Flat
Matteo

By the time Matteo had finally gotten through to his father, the old man had spoken to Don Alessandro and knew the game plan, the details of which Matteo wasn't privy to. And he didn't want to know. Living through and dealing with the aftermath of the violence directed at his brothers, his family, and the high-wire tension he'd endured for nine months was more than enough of being embroiled in the *family business* to last him a dozen lifetimes.

Most men born to that life would be disgusted with him, and he was all right with that. He didn't find any valor or virtue in violence. Sure, if someone came at him, he'd defend himself. He'd been involved in a couple of free-for-all pub brawls while at university. He'd trained and played on championship football teams for many years, and frequently ended a game bloodied and battered. His weekend games in London were friendly, but intense. He'd boxed at Cambridge, had learned to fence at Eton, and typically ran eight kilometers a day. Unlike the culture his family upheld, his definition of badass was to outsmart an opponent, not beat him to a pulp.

Now, sitting on his roof deck in his sweatshirt and track pants, sucking back a bottle of water after his morning run, Matteo absorbed the sounds and smells of his neighbourhood waking up, hoping the banality of everyday life would help bring him back to centre.

Finally, he'd begun work three weeks ago, and returning to his life had been akin to reentry to Earth after his spaceship had been on a three-year mission on another world. His mates acted as if he'd been gone a couple of weeks, making plans and expecting him to show up for all the activities in which he'd been engaged before. He'd jumped in with both feet, but felt a fog, or more like a barrier, between him and his friends, and the life he'd reassumed. They didn't seem to notice, but he knew he was, and always would be, apart from them. Separated by what he'd witnessed, had dealt with, and what he'd been expected to do.

For the rest of his life, he would see Mariano's mutilated body, his dick and balls cut off – they'd been stuffed in his mouth when he father had found his dead sons – his eyes carved out of his head, his torso a road map of bruises and knife wounds. And Due, a casualty of war, a bullet through his brain, a brother who'd had nothing to do with the horrible, terrible accident – a goddamn accident – that had taken Adriana and her unborn baby from her husband.

The requirement that two Parisis had to die to make up for – as if such an equation was thinkable – the La Rosas' lives lost was an abomination Matteo would never be able to reconcile.

The story, the make-believe of his brothers' boating accident and being lost at sea, meant no burial. With money and influence, their family undertaker – another reality of that world Matteo had a hard time wrapping his mind around, that a business was based solely on the dead the Parisis caused or suffered – made certain his brothers' cremation would remain a secret, their bodies reduced to ash to keep the fiction of their deaths solid.

The fuel in his engine, what kept Matteo together, was the calendar. In two months, he'd move to Boston. To Sofia.

On his first day at work, he'd requested and was granted a meeting with the managing partner, and asked if they'd move him to the Boston office. A swift yes was accompanied by genuine relief that "one of their own" would be able to keep an eye on what the "Yanks" were up to on the other side of the pond. Matteo had almost laughed at the imperious attitude many Brits still held about "the colonies."

Within a week, his estate agent had let Matteo's flat to a couple, both barristers newly accepted to Lincoln's Inn. The movers were coming on the last Wednesday in May to pack, organise, and take his things to storage. He'd be on a plane Friday, the cleaners were coming on Saturday, and the tenants would be in on Monday, June 1. The first day he'd be at work in Boston.

No word yet from Don Alessandro as to when Matteo would be able to speak to Sofia. Her safety was paramount, and as much as he longed to hear her voice, and see her via FaceTime, he'd wait until this hideous business was over and done with in a way it could never come back and hurt her. Until then, she'd continue to live in his fantasies every night, and frequently during the day. If he got to do half the things to and with her he imagined – and Matteo had a rich imagination – he'd die a happy man.

In the meantime, he'd connected with a couple of mates whose families were old money from Beacon Hill who'd sent their sons to Eton. Apparently, Exeter and Andover were beneath them. Carter and Gray were all over organising a flat for Matteo, who had four requirements: close to Tufts Fenway campus, an excellent kitchen, good plumbing, and heating. They undertook the task with diligence, and Matteo reached over for his iPad to look at the latest photos and floor plans the lads had sent over.

The neighbourhood that best fit his requirements, and put him close to work, was Back Bay. A little more than two kilometres to Tufts with bus and train connections, but he would collect Sofia from school. Not that he was opposed to mass transit, he used the tube in London all the time, but he wouldn't inconvenience her, and he relished the opportunity to be there to care for her.

As he sifted through the possibilities, one place caught his attention. An entire floor of a brownstone built in the 1880s was for sale that had three bedrooms, two baths, and a chef's kitchen. Modern tiled bathrooms, herringbone hardwood floors throughout, and custom built-ins and mouldings. They had one deeded parking space – he'd look into what that meant – and private storage. Nothing like the row houses in London, but that wasn't a bad thing. This place was newly renovated, modern with character, including the original bay windows and casements in the large living room and dining room area.

He shot off an email to Carter and Gray and set them about the business of being his representatives stateside.

Matteo could hear Sofia's chiding: *Why do you need a whole floor that's over two thousand square feet? And with three bedrooms and two bathrooms?*

Because, carina, *only the best for you.*

Di Caro Residence
Dutchford
Sofia

April showers might bring May flowers, but nowhere in that rhyme had anyone mentioned it bringing over a hundred people to their house. Easter was upon them.

Yesterday, Dad had gotten back from who knew where – although Sofia had her suspicions – and this morning their immediate family went to nine a.m. mass. As always, Sofia made sure she sat next to Nat. It'd become their thing: dinners, church, family gatherings, Sofia sat at the end of a row, couch, or in the last seat at a table, and Nat sat next to her. Which meant Gio was on the other side of Nat. Terrific buffer and support, plus Nat was a prankster, and a sly, cunning one at that.

This morning at breakfast, Ro was more impossible than usual. Snide remarks accompanied sneers during innocuous banter. Sofia saw the moment Nat had enough. Gio was complimenting *Nonna* on her *biscotti*, and Ro said, "Geez. You can buy the stuff everywhere. It's NBD." Uncharacteristically, *Nonna* took the hit and looked quashed. For a fleeting moment, Nat squinted at Ro, and Sofia knew it was game on.

Nat's first volley took place in the foyer. It'd been raining on and off, and every woman in the house knew better than to brave the outside marble steps in heels. There was a row of ugly rubber-sole booties in the front closet, and one by one, everyone grabbed their boots and slid their feet into them, their shoes tucked under their coats. When Ro yelled out, "Shit," Dad's brow went up, Mom's mouth pursed, and *Nonna* told Ro in Italian to watch her mouth. Ro pulled off a boot and tipped it over. Water dripped out, and before anyone could say a word, Ro ran upstairs to change her tights. The family that was noisy by definition waited in the limo in complete silence. Sofia figured Dad was too pissed to say anything, Mom and *Nonna* kept giving each other questioning glances, and Gio couldn't look at Nat.

Ro trudged into the car, barely giving them enough time to make it to mass. In the shuffle of getting seated in their pew, somehow, and Sofia couldn't figure this one out for the life of her, Nat had slipped bubble wrap under the pew pad exactly where Ro plunked down her butt. And, oh yeah, popping and snapping was happening for a couple of minutes until Ro figured out where the noise was coming from, and everyone in their row – of course they sat in the first pew – had to stand so Ro could extricate the bubble wrap.

By the time they sat down, Gio's head was buried in his Roman Missal while Nat remained composed with a butter-wouldn't-melt expression on her beautiful face. Services went off without any further incidents, and when they got home, they were all about helping get the house ready for the onslaught.

After the debacle at Thanksgiving when Aunt Bella lit into her son, Martin, everyone under the age of twenty-six sat together at one table – fifty-four people in the smaller of the two dining rooms at the more intimate, *don't laugh*, table, which was supposed to seat fifty people, but no one minded the minor squeeze – which left all the aunts, uncles, older cousins, and their young children to mentally wrestle with each other in the larger dining room at a table that sat seventy-five people, but there were only sixty-two in that room. This Easter's celebration should've included only Mom's side of the family, but for reasons known only to Sofia's folks, both sides were invited. Perhaps after Thanksgiving, they thought it wiser to dilute the gene pool, although both sides knew each other well, and had history.

Nat's hat trick came during dessert. Ro had recovered from her earlier embarrassments and probably figured the torment had run its course. With all the 'rents in another room, dinner was drama-free, and fun. The same company catered all the large Di Caro family events, and everyone had their favorites. When the dessert cart rolled in, the entire assemblage oohed and aahed. Ginormous platters filled with six different offerings were placed strategically down the center of the table. Ro was addicted to the *cannoli*, which had pistachio-infused ricotta cheese that gave the filling a light green tint. Absolutely yumalicious. Nat went around our end of the table, making a show out of using little tongs to put each type of pastry on everyone's plates. She had barely sat down when Ro screamed like someone had stuck her with a hot poker. Apparently, Nat had put copious amounts of wasabi in Ro's cannoli, and Ro never saw it coming because color-wise, the wasabi blended right in with the pistachio-infused filling.

After Ro had stuffed bread in her mouth and was able to form words again, Nat said, "Geez. I don't know what all the fuss is about. It's NBD."

Gio choked on his cheesecake, Sofia giggled, and Ro scowled, but didn't say a word.

Boston Back Bay
Matteo's New Home
Matteo

A universal fact: moving sucked. But for Matteo, relocating meant a new lease on life. He'd felt like a kid anticipating his first bicycle, or a teenager anxious about his first date. Since Tuesday, he hadn't slept more than three or four hours a night. By the time he boarded the plane, all he had to do was sit back and cross the Atlantic. But he found the flight painfully long, and no book, movie, or attempted nap could cure his excitement.

Carter and Gray collected him at Logan Airport and had him in his new home by 3:30 p.m. Carter had organised the WiFi, water, and utilities earlier in the week, and that morning, Gray had waited for the bed, bureau, and bedroom flat-screen to be delivered. Tomorrow the dining room table and chairs, and a large dove grey velour sectional sofa were scheduled to arrive in the early afternoon. Matteo didn't want to buy more than that without Sofia. He intended that this be her home too, and knew she'd want to put her personality into the décor.

As a thank you for being such spectacular mates, and with the intention of getting sozzled, Matteo booked a Lyft and took Carter and Gray to Sarma, a Middle Eastern restaurant that had come highly recommended in Somerville.

Now, after a morning run, and walking the 1.2 kilometers to his office, and learning in bad weather, when he took the bus, his commute would take no more than ten minutes, Matteo met his teammates. They were a group of about twenty people, a third of the size in the main office in London. He liked what he saw: camaraderie, support, and open communication. After the introductions and a brief meeting, Matteo was installed in his small, but functional office in Back Bay East, around the corner from the Old South Church. With so many choices of bakeries and cafés, he opted for *pain aux raisins* and a strong Americano from Flour Bakery + Café.

The city was smaller, the weather similar, the accents most decidedly different, but with all the conveniences he could want, Matteo felt he wouldn't miss London much at all. More importantly, at least for the next five years, he was home.

All he needed was Sofia.

122

Di Caro Residence
The Studio
Sofia

The knock on the door was too strong to be *Nonna*'s or Mom's. Sofia put aside the drawing she'd been bent over, and opened the door, expecting to see Gio, who was here for the weekend with Nat, of course. "Dad." She stepped back to let him in, surprised to see him home. For the past couple of months he'd been away as much as he'd been here, and she knew why, sort of. She could guess the reason, but not what he was doing. And she was certain she didn't want to know one thing about that *at all*.

He walked over to the drafting table, picked up her drawing, and studied the intricate, partially completed urban landscape. "You have a God-given talent. I'm pleased you're getting the recognition you deserve."

"Thanks," she mumbled. She wondered if she'd ever get comfortable with praise. He sat in her drafting chair, his feet flat on the floor. Hers barely made it to the first rung of the metal footrest. "What's up?"

He reached inside his suit jacket pocket, pulled out her phone, stretched out his arm, and placed it in her hand. "I took the liberty of programing in the phone numbers of the first person I suspect you're going to call."

She flung herself at him, hugging him around his neck at the same time she was gasping, laughing, crying on his shoulder. "Holy shit. Oh my god. I can't believe it," she chanted, banging the phone against his back in time with each word. Abruptly, she pulled away a few inches to see his lips twitching. "Everything is…is…all right?"

His bright blue eyes regarded her soberly. "Yes, sweet Sofia. Everything is all right."

She let out a long sigh. "I'm soooo glad."

"Me too."

He stood and she tugged his hand. "Thank you. Really."

"You're welcome. Really." He kissed the top of her head.

As he started to walk out of the studio, she clicked into her contacts and saw three phone numbers for Matteo: a cell and two office numbers, all of them with Boston area codes. "Hey," she called. "What's with the Boston digits?"

"I suggest you call and find out." He gave her his half grin, then turned and walked away.

Slowly, in a minor stupor, she closed the door and leaned against it. *Holy shit.* She hit Matteo's cell number and listened to it ring twice before he answered with, "Quick. Write down the time and date so we never forget when the rest of our lives began."

She began to cry but wrote the time and date on her drawing. "Wha...wha...what are...are...you doing in Boston?"

"Waiting for you, *cara.*"

Ten minutes into the call they hung up to switch to FaceTime, and Matteo spent the next half hour touring her around the place he bought in Back Bay less than a mile and a half from Tufts. Like an idiot, she started crying again, and as suddenly as she'd started, she stopped. "What are you doing right now?"

"Talking to you, Miff."

"Duh." She tilted her head and made a face at him. "I mean, do you have plans tonight? Tomorrow?"

"Nothing on. Just got back from a friendly football game. I need a shower and I'm good to go."

"Feel like driving down to Dutchford?"

"I thought you'd never ask."

***

Sofia locked up her studio, ran through the house into the family room where she expected to find Gio and Nat, but instead interrupted her parents doing the intimate whispering thing on the couch. She didn't have the brain space to process the lovey-dovey right now, and blurted out, "Matteo's coming for dinner and is staying over 'til tomorrow."

Her mother shifted her body to face Sofia and smiled. Her father leaned back, put his arm around her mother's shoulder, and brought her against his side. "We figured," she said. "*Nonna* took Ro and went to the market for fresh bread and vegetables." They didn't need fresh bread and vegetables. Ro had to be lectured before Matteo arrived, and no one was better to the task than the little general. "The guest bedroom opposite Gio's room is all made up for Matteo."

Across from Gio's room was a nice way of saying *on the opposite end of the hall from your room.* "Cool." Sofia turned on her heel and ran up the back staircase. She stuck her head in the guest bedroom across from Gio's room and saw a terry cloth bathrobe lying over the end of the bed. Hotel Di Caro. When she turned and saw Gio's door was closed, she didn't hesitate to knock, something she'd never do on any other day.

"Really, Soph?"

"How'd you know it's me?"

Gio flung the door open, his hair messier than bedhead. "Ro bangs with a flat hand. Mom and Dad call out, and *Nonna* would keep walking with her rosary in her hand if she saw the door closed. You rap lightly."

Sofia shook her head. "Whatever." She ducked under his arm, barged in, and told Nat, who was lying on her side somehow looking like a porno star while being fully clothed in a loose t-shirt and jeans, "Matteo will be here in like two hours. I need major wardrobe coaching."

"What?" Gio shouted behind her.

Nat righted herself and grinned. "Let's go."

"Hold up, Ace." He wrapped his arm around Nat's waist, stopping her progress through the room. "What the fuck, Soph?"

"He's living in Boston. Puh-leeeaze. I'm in crisis mode here. Long story later. 'Kay?"

Nat kissed his jaw, pulled away, and grabbed Sofia's hand.

***

"Are you sure?"

Nat was leaning against the headboard on Sofia's bed, legs crossed at the ankle. "Would I lie to you?"

Sofia slumped. "No. But I'm freakin' so all my fashion skills are on shutdown."

"Perspective," Nat announced. "He moved to Boston to be *with you.* Do you think he gives a shit what you're wearing when he finally gets to see you and touch you, after nine torturous months apart?"

"No." Sofia grinned, then took another look in the mirror. White round-neck cotton peasant blouse with flowery turquoise and orange stitching, long gauzy sleeves gathered at the wrist with orange thread, and turquoise-edged flouncy ruffle cuffs over wide-leg faded jeans, a turquoise scarf serving as a belt, its fringed edges hanging from a knot high on her left thigh. "Orange espadrille wedges or the white strappy sandals with the gold studs?"

Nat scooched to the end of the bed and peered over to look at Sofia's feet, on which were one of each shoe. "The espadrille. The color pops. You lose the sandals under the flared leg."

"Yeah." Sofia put one leg forward then the other to make sure. She went into the closet to her jewelry case and picked out two pair of earrings. Walking out, she held them up. "Dangly turquoise beads or oblong silver hoops?"

"Stick one in each ear." Sofia complied and turned her head, watching Nat's assessment. "I'm vibing the hoops. You?"

Sofia tilted her head to her left shoulder then her right, wishing she had a thick head of hair instead of the wispy see-through threads than hung to her shoulders. "Yeah. The hoops."

"A little mascara and lip gloss, and you're done, Soph. You don't need anything else."

"No bronzer? I'm pale as a ghost."

"If you want, add a couple of silver rings, but nothing else. You look like a boho princess."

Sofia sighed. "I'm sooo glad you're with my brother."

Nat flashed a wicked grin. "Me too."

***

5:15 p.m.

Sofia: Hey.
Amy: OMG. You got your phone back. Are you dancing on your bed?
S: No. I'm pacing up & down the main hall.
A: Ummm…okaaay. How come?
S: Matt's supposed to be here any minute.
A: Back the fuck up. How'd that happen?

S: Everything's cool now. He moved to Boston a couple of weeks ago. His firm transferred him. He's working in Back Bay, bought a place there, less than 1.5 miles from Tufts. I found out like three hours ago.
A: Holeee shit. What are you wearing?

Sofia took a photo from the neck down and sent it to Amy.

A: Excellent choice.
S: Nat picked it out.
A: So glad they're there. Help keep Nonna and Ro under wraps.
S: Nonna took Ro shopping as a pretense so she could give her a lecture.
A: If anyone can get through to the gansta, it's the general.
S: I fuckin hope so. I'm freaking so bad.
A: The minute you see him, you'll settle.
S: Shit. I think I hear a car.
A: LMK how it goes.
S: K

Sofia couldn't wait. She ran down the hall, threw open the front door, and froze. Matt, in a long-sleeve black button-down, the cuffs rolled halfway up his forearms, shirt tucked into faded jeans that rested on his hips like they were made to be there. He was getting out of a black Tesla with three huge bouquets clutched in his hand. He looked up, saw her, and smiled. One moment she was on the steps, the next she was plastered against him, her arms around him, his around her, the flowers resting against her neck and hair, the crinkle of their wrapping the backdrop to soft words whispered in her ear.

"So beautiful. I can't believe I'm holding you. *Tesoro mio.*"

Sofia's throat had constricted so tight she couldn't swallow, never mind speak, but who needed words. Matt was here. *Here.* She breathed in deep and took in his musky scent. Felt his broad solid chest beneath her cheek. Felt his incredible back muscles under her palms. Heard his heart thudding against her ear. She wanted to shout, dance, laugh, kiss him like crazy, and yet…she could stand wrapped in his arms for another six hours and be completely overjoyed.

Someone coughed, and reluctantly she stepped back to see her whole family standing on the landing of the front steps.

Matt lowered his head and muttered, "Be brave. It'll all be fine. I promise."

She looked up at his unbelievably handsome face and got lost in his caramel coffee eyes. He laced his fingers through hers and gave her hand a little shake before they walked to the front of the house and stopped on the step beneath the landing. Gently, he unwound their hands.

"*Donna Conti.*" He took *Nonna*'s hand and touched his lips to the back of it, then handed her a vibrant bouquet of fuchsia and orange Peruvian lilies. "*Piacere di conoscerla.*" From *Nonna*'s expression, she was pleased to meet him too.

"*Donna Di Caro.*" He clasped Mom's hand, released it, then offered her the bouquet of perfect peach roses. "Thank you for welcoming me to your home."

"I'm happy to finally meet you, Matteo." She gave him her big smile. The one she reserved for family.

Matt stuck out his hand then said, "Don Alessandro. An honour to be here, sir."

Dad shook Matt's hand but didn't say a word.

Matt turned to Nat. "Natalia. Sofia speaks highly of you."

Nat laughed. "She was buttering you up. Don't worry. You'll get used to us."

He grinned then stuck out his hand again. "Gio. Glad to meet you."

Gio clapped Matt on the back. "Bold, man." Then Gio winked at me.

Matt dipped his hand into the right front pocket of his jeans and pulled out something wrapped in yellow tissue paper. He handed it Ro. "For you, Aurora, so you'll always have good luck." She tore open the paper and inside was an oval glass pendant hanging from a silver chain. Embedded in the glass was a four-leaf clover.

Mom leaned over to look at it. "How lovely, Matteo. So thoughtful." Then she nudged Ro, who was looking at Matt with her mouth hanging open.

"Yeah. Really. I've never seen anything like this. Thanks."

Matt turned to Sofia and handed her the last bouquet: enormous violet roses. She looked up into his warm eyes and managed to croak out, "They're so pretty."

He smiled and nodded.

"*Basta*," *Nonna* ordered. "Inside. We have wine and antipasti waiting, and we need to put these beautiful flowers in water."

The first hurdle cleared and no one had been embarrassing, inappropriate, or bloodied.

A triumph.

Di Caro Residence
Kitchen Table
Matteo

The significance of eating at the Di Caros' kitchen table instead of in a formal dining room was not lost on Matteo. In anyone else's home, this kitchen table would be the formal dining table, but given the size of the house, and the scope of the Di Caros' entertaining – they had two formal dining rooms, each big enough for a state dinner with the Queen – this area was all about hearth and home.

Earlier, while *Nonna* and Francesca – she'd insisted he use her first name – went about the business of putting the flowers in water and arguing about where which bouquet would look best, Sofia gave him a tour of the house. She hadn't exaggerated when she'd told him her family could argue about anything. What she'd implied, and was obvious seeing it play out in front of him, their *arguments* were an affectionate, if not noisy, form of familial communication.

To say the Di Caro home was impressive gave new meaning to understatement. A few of the twenty-five rooms, not counting the ten bathrooms, were formal and tastefully elegant, filled with fine paintings and notable *objet d'art*. But most of the house was a family home filled with photographs and knickknacks of sentimental value rather than artistic. The rooms were spacious, but furnished to invite sitting and staying a while. His bedroom – he laughed when Sofia pointed out its location was at the opposite end of the hall from hers – was done in neutral light greys and blues, entirely suitable for any guest.

Security was tight, and obvious. The front entrance was gated, and he'd had to be screened before being let onto the long drive. A high solid wall surrounded the Don's considerable property, and from what Matteo could see, four men patrolled the grounds. Cameras were visible at the pool house, under the eaves of the main house, and in the trees. He surmised the security he didn't see was more sophisticated and deadlier.

During the tour, Sofia invited him to her graduation party with the caveat that hundreds of relatives would be there. She gave him an out, which he refused to take. Her graduation party was also her birthday party. Her eighteenth birthday. Matteo wouldn't miss giving her their first kiss on that momentous day for all the money in the world.

His restraint had been tested to its limits these past nine months. In her presence, he had to remind himself death awaited him if he inappropriately touched the Don's still-but-not-for-long underage daughter. Intentionally, Matteo had chosen to wear his tightest jeans. It hurt like a motherfucker when he got hard in these pants, and that *aide-mémoire* was just the thing to keep him in check.

In eleven days the handcuffs came off. After spending so much time imagining what he'd thought he couldn't have, then learned he could, but wasn't sure when, his control was near the breaking point. He'd promised himself he'd take it slow. Hell, they hadn't even had a first date. As much as he wanted her under him screaming his name when he was inside her, he'd force himself to be patient. He meant to keep her for the rest of their lives, and when they were celebrating their fiftieth wedding anniversary, he wanted her to remember that he'd courted her and always treated her like his *principessa*.

***

"Best Sicilian food I've ever had. I could eat a bucket of your pasta *alla Norma*."

At the same time *Nonna* blushed under Matteo's praise, Gio shouted, "Suck-up."

"Yeah," Ro added, "brownnose much?"

"Aurora," Francesca said *sotto voce.*

"What? Gio teases, it's okay. I say something and…"

Matteo saw Natalia squint at Ro. He had no idea what that meant, but it made Ro blanch. "Sorry," she mumbled.

"Quite all right. I admit freely to complimenting the chef. I want to be invited back." Matteo smiled at *Nonna* and winked at Ro.

"Go, sit." *Nonna* waved toward the family room. "Relax. I made something special for dessert."

Matteo made a show of holding his stomach. "I need to make room then. Anyone fancy a stroll?"

Gio laughed. "'Fancy a stroll'? Man, you're killing me."

Sofia giggled. She'd sat beside him during dinner and had made sure her thigh was pressed up against his during the whole meal. Sweet torture.

"I'll help *Nonna*." Natalia stood and motioned for Ro and Sofia to help. "You guys go have *a stroll*."

Gio grabbed Natalia around the neck and laid a wet one on her. Matteo was jealous of the casual intimacy and couldn't wait for the day he'd be able to have that with Sofia.

***

They walked to the pool house in companionable silence. Gio was a couple of years younger than Matteo, but clearly a contemporary. Comfortable in his own skin, friendly and incisive, had they met in school, they would've been mates. Perhaps they could be now. Not that Matteo needed internal allies: the Don's frosty demeanor notwithstanding, the family seemed happy to welcome him into the fold and appeared to accept that he belonged to Sofia.

Gio pressed a code into the keypad next to the French doors, and after a click, pushed his way into a room that did not say wet towels and plastic floating mattresses. Rattan furniture covered in bright flowers against a light green background was artfully arranged in a large room with a fireplace on the far wall. Large bamboo mats covered the *noce* tiled floors, and sturdy Polynesian-looking tables, carvings, and wall art were interspersed throughout the room. Hallways led off both sides of the main room, presumably to bedrooms and bathrooms.

Family photos framed in dark wood sat on top of a large chest of drawers behind the sofa. Matteo picked up what looked like a recent picture of Sofia surrounded by *Nonna*, Francesca, Ro, and Natalia, all looking at each other laughing.

Gio came up behind him and offered him a glass of whiskey. "Easter." He took a sip from his glass. "After the vultures left."

Matteo winged up a brow.

"Huge family. Some of them are great, others, I wouldn't miss. There were over a hundred people here for Easter dinner." He lifted his chin at the photo in Matteo's hand. "We were doing the postmortem and Mom, who never criticizes, let one slip about one of her sisters."

"The comment must've been spot-on."

Gio laughed. "Gotta tell you, man, you look more Italian than I do, but when you speak, I hear Dumbledore."

Matteo smiled as he put the picture back and took a sip of whiskey. The Don's extortionately expensive small-batch whiskey. "I went to Eton when I was thirteen, studied at Cambridge, and except for an occasional visit to Sicily, I spent nine years in England before returning to Vittoria for a few months. London is home. In most ways that matter, I'm more British than Sicilian."

"No shit." Gio grinned and moved to one of the couches. Matteo sat opposite him in a large wing chair. Gio didn't waste a moment. "Not to pry, and tell me to fuck off if you don't want to answer, but what was the deal in Sicily?"

If there was anyone in the world with whom he could share the truth, Gio fit the bill to a T. A Don's son with no interest or ambition to follow in the family business: a man making his way in the world on his own terms. A man in love and planning for a future that would approximate normal in a way that said *my name is not my legacy*. But Matteo wouldn't put the burden of the truth on Gio's shoulders. Bad enough Matteo had to carry that around the rest of his life.

He would never forget his father's groaning sobs when he received the phone call that his brothers were dead. He'd never forget seeing his father's face – the man had aged thirty years overnight – when he stepped off the family's plane in Sicily. He prayed he never again felt the carving hollow inside his body when he'd learned what had happened and why. Living months of enduring his father's near catatonic grief, then rage. Months of putting off the inevitable and not buckling under his father's pressure to *take care* of the matter once and for all. And that he'd had to give up Sofia to keep it from touching her had been more than his heart could bear.

He had no idea what Don Alessandro had done, but there were no reports of death or family warfare, and whatever the outcome, Matteo's father seemed satisfied with the result. Matteo would be eternally grateful to the Don for undertaking a responsibility he had never wanted. And by so doing, the Don had granted Matteo a life where he could love Sofia forever.

"I'm not telling you to fuck off. But I choose to keep you from shouldering a weight you don't need to carry." Gio's brow furrowed. "Suffice it to say, everything has been resolved in a way that Sofia will always be safe, and I didn't have to become a man I would have hated."

Gio blinked a few times. "Okay. Enigmatic, but good to know my sister is a priority." Matteo nodded. "So, you ready for this?"

"This being…"

"Everything Di Caro."

"Ah. Well, as I'm sure you've surmised, the backdrop of your father's business is familiar, but unlike you, I didn't grow up immersed in it. I'm ten years younger than my next oldest brother was, and spent most of my early years influenced more by my mother than my father. After she died, quite intentionally, my father didn't want me to live in that world and sent me to England to travel a different path."

Gio nodded. "Couldn't imagine Soph with anyone in *the life*. Not my thing, and way far from hers."

Matteo took this opportunity to steer the conversation away from his near miss in getting sucked into a life based on revenge, destruction, and death, which would've meant he'd never have Sofia. "She told me you want to be a medical doctor."

"Yeah. I'm a little late to the game. I have one more required class to take this fall. I'm sitting for the MCAT in March. Means, if I get in, I have a gap year between college and medical school."

"Not a bad thing to take a break. I've heard it's intense. Any plans for the year?"

"Soph knows, but keep it under wraps." Matteo tilted his chin. "Nat and I will be travelling. Doing a six-month honeymoon before the wedding."

"All in, then."

"Knot's tight, bro."

"Happy for you, Gio."

"Thanks, man."

"Let me know where you're heading. I'll give you contacts along the way. Lots of mates live far and wide."

"'Preciate it." He twirled his glass around on his knee, looking pensive before he lifted his head, as if he'd made a decision. "Not trying to be the doomsday guy, but our family can be a bit much."

Kind of him to try to prepare Matteo for what was coming. "Sofia calls it dramarama."

Gio laughed and seemed relieved Matteo was taking it in stride. "Perfect description."

"I'm looking forward to meeting Toni and Aaron's brood. I've heard they're favorites of yours."

"The best. And atypical of the rest, fair warning."

"I've heard this too."

"You'll be okay. Nat says she takes it in like theater or performance art. Mostly, she's entertained."

"Good advice."

They'd come to an understanding. Sofia's big brother approved of her choice and would back her man if the situation warranted. Matteo kept his secrets, but promised Sofia was his everything.

They finished their drinks and carried their glasses back to the main house.

***

After dessert, an extraordinarily rich *cassata Siciliana*, and much-needed *espresso*, the Don, Francesca, and *Nonna* absented themselves, leaving Ro, Natalia, Gio, Sofia, and Matteo to play a vicious game of Monopoly, made so by Ro, who would settle for nothing less than world domination. When the game was over, Gio and Natalia dragged Ro upstairs.

Alone with his Sofia for the first time since that fateful night nine months ago, Matteo took her in from head to toe. She was dressed casually, but fashionably. Walking along the King's Road, he'd seen many young women in clothes much like hers, but on her the garments took on an ethereal quality, as if the clothes would flutter around her and become wings. Poetic nonsense, but he was so lost in her delicate beauty, he felt sure he could paint her with the skill of Renoir.

She gave him a sweet smile as she stood, then went across the room and docked her phone. A few moments later, Harry Styles's "Lights Up" came through speakers Matteo, which must've been placed throughout the space. She motioned to him, and when he joined her in an open area between the family room and the kitchen table, she walked into his arms and they began to sway. Her cheek hit him mid-chest, and given his height, he had to dip his chin to rest it on the top of her head. Her hair smelled like sunshine, and when he enveloped her lithe body in his arms, she burrowed in, no space between them now.

She raised her head and whispered, "Eyes and ears everywhere."

He'd suspected the Don had the interior of his house monitored. "Surely, not the bathrooms," he teased.

He felt her smile against his chest. "No, but there are cameras in the bedrooms."

"I can't imagine Gio allows that."

She tilted her head up and he took in her magnificent smile. "He made sure the one in his room was switched off."

"I bet he did."

She grinned. "If we want to talk, outside is best," she continued to whisper as Taylor Swift's "Lover" ended and "Dancing With A Stranger" started. "If we talk low, and keep walking, the mics don't pick up much."

At the same time she loosened her arms, he stepped back, and then laced his fingers with hers. They walked past the pool and pool house along a flagstone path that wended through a large rose garden.

"I'm having a hard time believing you're here." She clasped her fingers tight in his hand.

"Here and not going anywhere without you, Miff."

Her cheeks flushed and she glowed. "Do you like Boston?"

"There's a lot packed into a small city. Plenty of distractions and entertainment, and I found a good weekend football game. No complaints."

"You like your job? Is it the same as in London?"

"The work is the same. The office is smaller, which I prefer. The team seems cohesive and supportive. It's fine, really."

She yanked on his hand. "You're not just saying that?"

"You have a pretty good bullshit detector. You tell me."

She scrutinized his face for a moment, then shook her head. "Yeah. I'm getting the truth."

He grinned and thought their kids weren't going to get away with much, and he felt sorry for them already. While she probably wouldn't agree, she had a lot of *Nonna* in her.

"You wanna hear something funny?" she asked.

"Ha-ha funny or peculiar?"

"Both actually." He nodded. "Amy and I booked a trip to Canada based on your travelogue letter, which I hated by the way. I knew what you were doing."

He stopped her and made her look at him, not caring if the Don heard every word. "Think, Miff. Put yourself in my shoes. Aside from breaking a promise to your father, which I loathed doing, I knew I couldn't have you, would never see you again, and, most importantly, I *had to* keep you safe." He leaned down so his face was close to hers. "Had. To." He pulled back a little. "In fairness to you, the best thing I could do was to push you away. I wanted you to be angry with me, forget me, and move on with your life."

She pulled her hand out of his and took a step back with her fists balled. "Do you think I'm so shallow that I'd forget what happened that night?"

"Christ, no."

"Then what the fuck, Matt? A few letters emphasizing the distance between us didn't push me away, it pissed me off and hurt my heart."

"No more than it hurt mine." She looked chastised. He reached for her hand and she let him weave their fingers together again. "I'm not brushing it aside as if it didn't matter, but those shitty nine months are in the past. I'm here. We're together. Let's go forward, okay?"

"Okay," she whispered.

"You should go to Canada."

"Are you serious right now?" She pulled her hand away again. "Ten minutes after I got you back, you want me to go away for six weeks?"

He grinned at her and she looked like she wanted to smack him. "Think, Miff."

"I'm thinking you need your head examined."

He couldn't help it, he laughed.

"What's so fuckin' funny?"

He leaned down and whispered, "How old are you going to be when you step on that plane?"

Her eyes widened.

"During the week, I have work. I'm new. I need to prove my worth. I have to put in the hours. That means late nights. But the weekends…" He saw the minute the light went on in her head.

"When I'm travelling, I'll be in a hotel."

He nodded.

"And you can meet me wherever we are."

He nodded some more.

"And," she whispered really low, "we can be together."

He tapped his forefinger against his temple.

"Oh my god, you're brilliant."

"So I've been told."

"And arrogant."

"That too."

She shook her head as if she was scolding him. Yeah, their kids were going to catch it. "You know, we're supposed to leave the day after the graduation party."

"Then go."

Her eyes widened and she smiled. "I have a great idea." He waited. "Stay the night of the party, and drive us to the airport in the morning." Before he could respond she asked, "Would it be okay if you got into work late?"

"It would, and you're right, it's a good idea."

She got close and stood on her tiptoes so she could whisper in his ear, her warm breath a tease against his neck, "We're leaving on Thursday. Can you be in Montreal on Saturday?"

He whispered back, his face buried in her soft hair, "Absolutely."

She grabbed his hand and said, "Get ready for a shit-ton of FaceTime during the week."

Gently, he squeezed her fingers. "I'm counting on it."

Di Caro Residence
Sofia's Room
Sofia

12:27 a.m.
S: You up?
A: Duh. I've been waiting forever. What happened, and don't leave anything out.
S: Come for brunch tomorrow.
A: Regular time?
S: Yeah. 11:15.
A: I'm there.

***

Weird and so right. That's how Sofia felt being bracketed by Matt on her left and Nat on her right. He was the last seat in the pew. *Nonna* was on the other side of Gio, Ro wedged between *Nonna* and Mom, and Dad, as always, at the end of the row, closest to the main aisle.

Protected and comfortable. People who knew and loved her were watching out for her, and while Nat couldn't give a rat's ass – her words – about religion, she came to Mass with them because she was family. Matt grew up in the church, though he admitted that during his years at Cambridge he'd gone to church only for weddings. He had to attend when he was in Sicily. It'd been expected, but he didn't care if he never went again. But here he was beside her because he was family now too. Nat didn't know the liturgy and didn't say anything that wasn't written down in front of her, and she never sang. Matt knew it all, Latin and English. *Nonna*, who bobbed her head forward a couple of times to see down the row, noticed and beamed. Whatever. It made certain family stuff easier, but it didn't change a thing. He was hers and she was never letting him go.

Of course, after Mass, the minute they hit the landing outside the front door, *Nonna* made a fuss when introducing Matt to Father Ursini, speaking in Italian, gesturing broadly. Everyone stood at the bottom of the steps waiting until the show was over. Sofia rolled her eyes at Nat, who reminded her this was a good thing. "Could you imagine how many rings of hell your life would be if she didn't like him?" Sofia shivered at the thought.

They got home a little after 10:30 and a flurry of activity commenced. As she did every Sunday, *Nonna* baked fresh *brioche* early, letting it cool on the counter while they were at Mass. The scent of lemon-infused baked goods hung in the air when they entered the kitchen, and it smelled fantastic. *Nonna* went straight to the kitchen, Sofia and Nat joined her, Gio roped Matt into setting the table: a favor really, otherwise he would've had to make small talk with Ro and Dad.

Nonna got busy with the baked eggs with artichokes, *burrata*, spinach, and spicy tomato sauce, while Mom made *panna*. Later, she'd crack the lemon *granita* and stuff it and the *panna* into the brioche. Sofia and Nat cut up fruit and made a giant fruit bowl.

They were laying out the food on the kitchen table when the doorbell rang. Ro answered it and came back with Amy, who stopped so fast she jolted, and her eyes went so wide her brows nearly disappeared in her hairline.

As Sofia approached her immobile friend, she called, "Ames?"

Amy seemed to come out of her trance and whispered, "He's a god."

Sofia laughed and yanked on Amy's hand. "Let me introduce you."

Amy refused to budge. "No, really. He's not normal. No one is that gorgeous."

"He is, and he's waiting to eat. Come say hello."

Amy allowed Sofia to drag her to Matteo. "Matt, this is Amy. Amy, Matt."

He stuck out his hand. "Pleasure to finally meet you."

She shook two of his fingers, like that was all she could manage. "Ah...me...too."

He looked at Sofia, who dragged Amy to her chair. "Is she all right?" he asked.

Sofia told Amy, "Sit. Drink water." Then turned to Matt and said, "You made an impression." He grinned. Sofia sat and pointed to the seat next to her. "Don't get cocky. It's not a good look on you."

He lowered himself in the seat next to her and leaned in, "I thought you liked the way I look."

"You have your moments."

Nonna planted her butt in her chair across from Matt and told everyone, "*Mangia.*" Dad sat at the head of the table, natch, Mom always to his left, Ro to his right. Gio and Nat sat across from Sofia and Amy.

As Amy spooned fruit into the small bowl on her plate, she whispered to Sofia, "This is weirding me out."

Sofia took the fruit salad and spooned some into her little bowl, then passed the fruit to Matt. "Huh?"

"Everyone's acting like he's a foregone conclusion."

Sofa finished chewing a piece of cantaloupe. "He is."

Amy gave her big eyes.

"Tomorrow," Sofia whispered. "I'll give you the whole story in school tomorrow. Now be cool."

Amy nodded and put a piece of honeydew in her mouth.

***

Sofia and Matt were lying out by the pool under a huge umbrella. Matt had insisted on the shade. He'd worried about her being in the sun even with sunscreen.

Amy had left around two, cursing and storming off after Monica called and was probably her usual bitchy self.

"What was that about?" Matt asked after Amy left.

"Monica," Sofia answered. "Amy's bitch of a mother. She treats Amy like shit. Always has. Right now she's on a rant because she's pissed Amy's going to Canada."

"If she doesn't like her, why is she annoyed Amy is going away?"

"You're too logical. Monica's twisted. She wants her daughter to be as miserable as she is. When Amy's in Canada, Monica can't torture her. Being with me makes it worse. Monica is not a fan."

"Who wouldn't like you?"

"You're biased."

"Clearly." He gave her a lazy smile. "Sounds awful for Amy, though."

"It sucks. Insult to injury? Amy's eighteen already and has her own money, courtesy of her grandmother on her father's side. The grandma hates Monica and set up a trust fund for Amy for when she turned eighteen, which was two months ago. After Amy gets back from Canada, she's spending most of August with her grandmother at her house in the Hamptons. When Ames gets back, she's moving into the dorms at BU the first day she can, which is a week before classes start. After that, I don't think she'll ever go home again."

"What about her father?"

"He's still married to Monica, but he's hardly around. He travels a lot for business, but everyone knows that's an excuse. Amy thinks he has a mistress and spends most of his time with her."

"I'm guessing division of assets is the reason he hasn't divorced Monica."

"That's what Amy thinks. I think he's a shit. He leaves Amy alone three weeks out of four with Monica knowing how she is and how she treats their daughter. Who does that?"

"A shit."

"Damn straight."

***

Matt left after dinner. Sofia hated that he had to go, and she wished she could at least kiss him good-bye. All weekend she'd done everything she could to touch him, mostly surreptitiously, so as not to send her father into paroxysms. She'd agreed to FaceTiming during the week, and they'd made plans for him to come down on Friday evening, spend the night, then on Saturday morning they'd go to Providence and hang out with Gio and Nat. Sunday, they'd have their first official solo date. Matt wouldn't tell her where they were going, but he promised she'd love it.

About ten minutes after Matt had left, Gio and Nat said their good-byes, and the house felt empty. Sofia went to her studio but couldn't concentrate on her piece. She sat at the edge of her chair, leaning on her drafting table, replaying every minute with Matt. Every touch, every facial expression, the sound of his voice, and damn, his incredible body on display in Gio's swim trunks. That she didn't jump him was a miracle. But she did get some satisfaction, though not the kind she wanted, when every half hour or so, he went into the cold pool and stayed there for about ten minutes.

He'd done nothing to hide his regard when she took off her wrap and lay on the longue in her one-piece, and his face kept turning in her direction all afternoon. She couldn't see his expressive eyes behind his shades, but she imagined he was devouring her. She certainly felt like it when his breathing became rapid and he went into the pool.

She was still in her Matt fog when she got a text.

M: Sitting in traffic. A construction mess on I-90.

S: There's always a mess on I-90. Be careful.

M: We're starting to move again. I'll call you when I get home.

S: K.

Home. She couldn't wait until that meant where they both lived.

Near Brown University
Providence
Matteo

Considering the magnitude of all the secrets Matteo had lived with, and the ones he'd never share, especially not with Sofia, keeping Gio and Natalia's new flat under wraps was a miniscule favor.

When they pulled up in front of a house a few blocks away from Brown University's campus, Sofia asked, "What are we doing here?"

"It's the address your brother texted."

"Huh." She shrugged. "Weird. Let's go in."

They went up to the second floor of the small building that looked like it had been a private home at one time, and knocked. Natalia answered barefoot, wearing yoga pants and a Brown t-shirt.

"Hey, you found us. Come in." She stepped forward and gave them both a big hug, then stepped back from the door and motioned them in with her hand.

They walked into a new or remodeled flat with a decent-size lounge that had a comfy-looking tan sofa, a big flat-screen on a short entertainment unit, and a coffee table. Ahead and to the left was a round glass kitchen table with four chairs, and beyond the eating area was a fully equipped kitchen with new appliances and all the modern conveniences. Off the lounge were three doors. Nat directed them to the door closest to the front of the flat, opened it, and waved them into a small bedroom with a double bed covered with a tan comforter, next to which was a nightstand, and across the room, a small three-drawer bureau. "This is your room."

Matteo's heart thudded against his rib cage. Four days until Sofia's eighteenth birthday. No way was he jumping the gun. For months she'd been featured in his every fantasy. For weeks he'd waited, counting the days until he could finally see her. Everything was riding on him keeping his word, and he would. He *had* to wait until she was legal no matter what his dick was telling him.

Sofia turned and grinned at him.

Fuck.

Natalia walked back to a short hall and they followed. "This is the bathroom." She opened the door to a small but new-looking three-piece with a white tiled shower stall. Clean and functional, but not much room to move around.

"This is our room." She showed them the bigger bedroom at the end of the hall with a queen-size bed shoved against one wall covered in a dark blue comforter. Four large pillows with white shams leaned against the wall where a headboard should be, and a small nightstand stood beside the bed. A bureau of six drawers was against the opposite wall next to the closet, and a small wooden desk and its swivel chair were against the far wall.

A first flat with all the necessities: comfortable, but not plush. Matteo had to hand it to Gio. He was carving out his life without relying on his family's notoriety.

They were all walking back into the lounge when Gio came in the front door carrying two white plastic bags. The scent of delicious Asian food filled the room. "Hey." He smiled. "Thai." Natalia went to him and kissed him on the mouth. Gio leaned into her and deepened the kiss for a quick moment before lifting his head and smiling at her. Then she grabbed one bag and he followed her into the kitchen with the other, placing it on the counter. "Sit." He waved his hand at the table. "We'll put everything out, and then we'll go for it."

"Gio," Sofia called. He turned around and looked at his sister. "Where are we?"

"Our new apartment. You like?"

"Well, yeah. It's cool. But... You're not going back to the quad?" He shook his head, and Sofia looked stunned. "What about the extension?"

On the way down to Providence, Matteo had heard all about Gio's quad-mates, their personalities and their pranks. She'd explained in detail how Gio and his roommate Howie had cut out a door between Natalia's room and the quad, making her room a quad extension, and that they'd gotten away with it all year.

"We took down the door, redid the drywall, painted, and the extension is now in the annals of history."

"Why?"

Gio and Natalia carried all the cartons to the table, then brought plates, napkins, chopsticks, spoons, and forks. "What do you want to drink?" Gio asked. "We got beer, sparkling water, apple juice, red wine, and regular water."

"Beer," Matteo replied.

"Sparkling water," Sofia said.

"Glass or bottle?" Gio held up two beers.

"Bottle's fine," Matteo answered.

Natalia brought a big bottle of sparkling water and two glasses to the table, and sat. Gio sat next to her a moment later, tops off the beers. He handed one to Matteo then turned to Sofia. "Nat and I have monster class loads in the fall and I have to start studying for the MCATs. Evan and Ashley moved into their own place. He took the MCATs already and was accepted at Albert Medical School. They're not leaving Providence anytime soon. Howie wants a single for his senior year, and boom, the quad broke up. Even if everyone had stayed, I need the quiet. I gotta focus. Much easier to do in our own space."

"What's the big secret? Why didn't you say anything last weekend?"

"Have you met *Nonna*?"

Sofia laughed. "Ah, yeah."

"Mom and Dad aren't stressing over Nat and me living together. They know. *Nonna*? I'm thinking she'd be on the rosary nonstop, and she'd drive everyone crazy with the going to hell and sin stuff."

"Least said soonest mended," Matteo stated.

"Exactly," Natalia said. "Why stir her up?"

"Ro doesn't know either." Gio picked up his chopsticks and pulled some Pad Thai onto his plate. "Not because Mom and Dad are worried about her getting ideas. They know she's a gansta. They're keeping it under wraps cuz she won't be able to keep her mouth shut."

"Back to *Nonna* finding out." Sofia put a spring roll on her plate.

Matteo spooned green papaya salad on his plate. "What's going to happen when you take off during the gap year?"

"We'll be much closer to the wedding, maybe she won't get quite so beside herself," Natalia replied.

"Hey." Sofia looked at everyone. "You two sleep together in our house."

"And every time we get ready to leave, *Nonna* pulls me aside and tells me the Lord might forgive me, but she won't until I marry Nat. Then she tells me to go to confession."

***

Sofia

After food, everyone wanted to take a walk, but it'd started to rain hard, so they stayed in. When the guys put on some Japanese ancient warrior kung-fu-type movie, Sofia and Nat went into her and Gio's room.

"You happy about this?" Sofia waved her hand at the room as she moved to the center of the bed and crossed her legs yoga style.

"Thrilled," Nat replied. "The quad was fun, and we had a room to ourselves, but every trip – food, TV, the bathroom – required we share our space. I'm not a fan of a thirty-person communal bathroom, even if there were four toilets, sinks, and showers."

"Totally understandable."

"We've got a little laundry room in the basement here. There are only eight apartments in the building, which means no giant backlog, broken machines, or soap gunk. I know, I sound so bougie, but I'm okay with it. I like my creature comforts."

"I think it's safe to say, compared to me, you're a survivalist."

Nat laughed. "Yeah, well, get used to the living on the kibbutz, sistah, you're three months away from dorm life."

Sofia looked down and started plucking at the comforter. "Um, yeah. About that."

Nat leaned in and stuck her face under Sofia's. "Talk to me."

She took a deep breath and lifted her head. "Matt bought this amazing place in Back Bay, and I want to live there with him."

"Does he know that?"

"Not yet. I thought I'd wait until we were in bed together."

Nat let out a long sigh. "Not a bad plan. They're so pliable after. But let's break this down." Sofia waited for Nat's wisdom. "I'm guessing he hasn't even kissed you yet."

"Sad, but true."

"Put yourself in his shoes. Would you want to fuck with your father on the whole eighteen-and-legal thing?"

"No. And it's why I think I'm gonna get pushback on living together."

"You have to know your father isn't going to like it."

"I do. And I thought about it. Really, I have. I'll be in class, the library, a study group, a studio, or the museum, sixteen hours a day or more. I could do the whole dorm room fiction, but I'm going to go to Matt's every night no matter what. Doing the sneaking around is bullshit. I'm so over being told what's good for me, I could scream."

"I get you, truly. But here's the thing, perception is as important as reality. If anyone could understand what being sure of her own mind at eighteen means, it's me. But I didn't have your background, and the expectations of a family that loves you. I know you feel suffocated right now, but in a few days you'll be in Canada. And I'd bet this rock," she fisted her left hand and pushed her engagement ring toward Sofia, "that a week from today, you and Matt will be horizontal in a hotel room in Montreal."

"God, we better be," Sofia stated. "I'm crawling out of my skin."

Nat grinned. "Imagine how he must feel."

"I don't need to imagine it. Last weekend he went into the pool about every half hour to cool down his hard-on."

Nat cracked up. "Poor dude."

"Poor me," Sofia huffed. "That temptation was a few feet away from me for hours."

Nat patted Sofia's knee. "Soon, sunshine. Hang tough."

Sofia grunted.

"For what it's worth, I recommend living the fiction for a year. Make it look like your staying at the dorm. Give your folks and *Nonna* the opportunity to help you set up your room, meet your roommate, walk around campus, do the proud family thing. After you have your freshman year under your belt, you'll seem older and more mature to them. I know it doesn't make any sense, but parents need the adjustment more than their kids do. You can move in with Matt the summer after your freshman year. They might not like it, but they'll be less beside themselves than if you do it now."

Sofia hung her head. "I know you're right, but I hate it."

"Honey." Sofia lifted her head at Nat's warm tone. "You'll be with him anyway. An idea." Sofia nodded. "You wanna be smart about it, get another phone. Keep the one you have with you when you're on campus, and when you get ready to leave for Matt's put your family phone under your mattress in the dorm. This way, your father can derive some satisfaction when he checks up on your whereabouts at night."

"You know about that?"

"Please."

"Huh. I'm beginning to think Ro acts all gansta, but you're the real-deal badass."

Nat batted her eyelashes. "You don't know the half of it."

***

The rain had stopped a few minutes after the movie was over. They put on their shoes, and headed out to walk Fox Point. After meandering in and out of shops, Gio took them to The Wild Colonial Tavern, which was in one of Rhode Island's oldest buildings. Even Matt said it reeked of hundreds of years of ale. They shared some spicy – as in burn your tongue – hummus and pita, the guys got ale and Reuben sandwiches, and Nat and Sofia had the vegan chili over chips, which was fantastic.

As they were heading back to Gio and Nat's place, Matt tugged on Sofia's hand, which he'd held all evening, and they hung back a bit.

"What?" she asked.

Matt bent down and whispered in her ear, "I'm going to sleep on the couch tonight."

Sofia turned her head and saw the conflict in his caramel coffee eyes. "I figured." She sighed.

"One week, Miff." He squeezed her fingers.

"I hope I don't spontaneously combust before then."

He threw back his head and laughed.

***

Matteo

The sofa was comfortable, but he couldn't sleep for more than a couple of hours at a time. By seven in the morning, he'd had a shower, made coffee, and was fully dressed, sitting at the kitchen table, reading the news online.

Sofia stumbled out of the bedroom, adorably disheveled and engulfed by his t-shirt, which came down to her knees. She glanced at the couch, then her gaze moved to the table. When she saw him she smiled, and damn, he felt that in his throat, his heart, and his dick. He marvelled at her effect on him, and gave up trying to understand it. After replaying over and over every moment of their encounter in that back hallway in a small *pasticceria* in Vittoria, he'd come to believe some hand, a fate, or something divine, had interceded and brought her to him. However it happened, and whatever it was that had given him the gift she was, he would spend the rest of his life honouring it.

She shuffled over to him, stood between his legs, put her arms around his shoulders, and rested her cheek on the top of his head. "G'morning," she muttered as he splayed his fingers around her tiny waist.

"You sleep?" he asked her shoulder, taking in her sweet warmth and light scent. No perfume, but somehow his Sofia always smelled like flowers.

"Not much. You?"

"Same."

"Sucks."

"Indeed."

"Shower then coffee."

"Here." He lifted his cup.

She looked down and scrunched her nose. God, she was cute. "You don't put anything in it."

"Unadulterated."

"Thanks, *Signore Espresso*, but I'll make my own after I get dressed." She stepped back, turned, and shuffled to the bathroom, her tiny arse barely visible beneath his shirt.

By the time she was dressed and ruining her coffee with milk and sugar, Gio came into the kitchen wearing only a pair of jeans. "Yo," he muttered. Apparently, the Di Caro siblings didn't spring out of bed all bright eyed and bushy tailed. He looked at her coffee and asked, "How can you drink that swill?"

"Not you too," she snapped.

He grabbed a mug and poured himself some coffee. After his second sip he said, "Ahhh. The fog is clearing." Sofia looked up at her brother, and Matteo couldn't see one iota of family resemblance.

Gio was a bit taller than Matteo, which made him a full foot taller than Sofia. Dark hair and olive skin, Gio was his father all over. Taller and more muscled than his dad, but no one could mistake his parentage. Sofia favored her mother, but was a softer, smaller, more delicate version. Matteo had learned quickly that in Sofia's case, looks were truly deceiving. There was nothing delicate about her fierce spirit. That was something she shared with her brother in spades.

"Nat still sleeping?" she asked.

"Shower," Gio told his cup before taking another long sip.

When Nat came into the kitchen fully dressed and looking more awake than all of them put together, Sofia was plating up scrambled eggs and toast. Blueberries and yoghurt were on the table in bowls at each place setting.

"Wow." Nat sat down and watched Sofia carry the plates with eggs and toast over to the table. "Wanna come down every weekend and do breakfast?"

"Bit of a schlep from Boston to Providence." Sofia sat and dug into her yoghurt.

"True." Nat nodded. "Maybe we can switch off."

Sofia licked her spoon and Matteo near came in his pants. "When we're not cramming, you're on. September in Boston."

Near Brown University
Providence
Matteo

He'd had the whole day planned out. Their first official date was supposed to be an early lunch at The Duck and Bunny, but without dessert, because they were going to head over to the WaterFire Arts Center for the Great Cupcake Championship. Instead they wound up having the kind of intimate conversation with Gio and Nat no Brit would ever have. Without warning, and apropos of the nothing important they'd been discussing over breakfast, Nat asked Sofia, "You have birth control covered?"

Gio's lip curled into a snarl. "Am I supposed to sit here and listen to you talk about that with my sister?"

Nat rolled her eyes. "Who are you right now?"

Gio pointed at his chest. "The guy you live with, remember?"

"Exactly," Nat said as if that covered everything. When Gio gave her a blank look, she shook her head and explained, "We've been shacked up since the day I stepped off that plane. Pot and kettle, baby. They're going to be in the same situation. Pretending that isn't going to happen makes you sound like your grandmother."

"Harsh, Ace."

"You can deal." Nat grabbed his hand and linked their fingers. Then she turned to Sofia again. "So?"

"I'm on the pill," Sofia answered.

Matteo had presumed she hadn't slept with anyone, and before he could check his reaction, he blurted, "Why?"

She turned her head slowly, her brows drawn together. "You ever use condoms?"

He sat back in his chair so fast it moved. "How is that relevant?" At that point, Nat and Gio got up and went down the hall to their room.

"Are you a virgin, Matt?"

He leaned forward and squinted at her. "I'm nearly twenty-three years old, Miff."

"I'll take that as a no."

"Correct. No."

She crossed her arms over her chest and stared at him. Fuck. He didn't want to have this conversation ever, but especially sitting in this small flat where Gio and Nat could hear every word. In for a pence... "And you?"

"Me what?" she gritted out. He almost clarified, but she put up her hand. "You know, let's not do this. I don't see how anything that happened before we became us is relevant."

Bloody hell. All those months ago he'd kept his hands and mouth to himself because of her age and apparent innocence. When he'd left her that morning all those months ago, his balls had been so blue he'd felt like he needed to soak in an ice bath. And now, he'd been waiting to kiss her, insisting that she be eighteen: legal and the age of consent. But what really had his gut churning was thinking that someone else had touched her before him. He knew that made him the worst kind of sanctimonious shithead, and yet he couldn't help how he felt. She was his and his alone.

"Quite right," he replied, keeping his tone as even and neutral as possible.

She stood, glared at him, and said, "I'm going to take a shower." Then she stomped into the bedroom, came out a few minutes later with her clothes tucked under her arm, and stomped into the bathroom.

A couple of minutes later Gio and Nat came out of their room. Nat leaned down and squeezed Matteo's shoulder. "I'm so sorry. I had no idea I was stirring up a hornet's nest."

Matteo shook his head. "My fault, not yours. My mouth moved before my brain fully connected."

Gio laughed. "According to Nat, I do that all the time." She nodded. "Don't stress. It's not fatal."

"Not yet, anyway." Nat gave Gio a sidelong stare that could crack marble. To Matteo she said, "I know you had the whole day planned out, but you might want to give me some time with Soph alone."

He hated that the day had blown up, but if anyone could set Sofia to rights about such a touchy subject, Nat could. "I'm thinking that might go over better."

"You guys do your thing, and I'll text later. Let's plan on having an early dinner before you head north."

Matteo nodded, and Gio clapped him on the back.

Fucking brilliant.

***

Sofia

They were almost nose-pressing the glass, peering into The Duck and Bunny. "This is where he was going to take me to lunch?"

Nat smiled. "Yeah."

"He's really sweet.

"He is."

Sofia wanted to kick herself. Her reaction to his "Why?" had been militant, and she'd felt that in her soul. She'd been offended that he'd asked. As if he had a right to question what she did with her body.

Sofia turned and faced Nat. "Am I delusional? I mean, maybe he's like all those other Sicilians and I'm blinded by his British veneer."

Nat cracked up and linked her arm with Sofia's, dragging her down the street. "You're not delusional. He's in love and he wants you all to himself. Guys say and do stupid things all the time, even the best ones. From everything I've heard, he had a great mom who died too young to impart some important lessons. He went to boarding school and college far from home, and had an absent father and brothers he barely knew. You're the one who's going to have to guide him to be more mindful."

"Ugh."

"It's a good thing. Really. *Nonna*, who is full of advice, some of it even good, told me how you let your husband treat you in the first month of marriage is how he'll behave through the whole marriage. Since I got a jump on the marriage part, I'm working it with your brother, who, as you know, is a wonderful person. But he's still a guy, and that thing between his legs controls his thought processes and behavior, especially when it comes to me. Matt is no different."

Now Sofia was second-guessing herself. "Did I overreact?"

"Nope. You fell down on the follow-through."

"Shit."

"You're new at this. You'll learn. The most important thing is to talk it out, fight it out, whatever works for you two. Gio and I have had some humdingers."

"I know," Sofia said. "I heard you fighting at Christmas and I thought you were breaking up cuz it sounded so intense."

Nat squeezed Sofia's arm. "Everything we do is intense." *That's what Theresa said.* "But we don't let shit sit and fester. You guys shouldn't either. Get it out, deal, and move on."

Sofia tugged on Nat to stop them. "I'm not like you. You're fearless."

"Ha," Nat barked out. "Hardly. But when it comes to your brother, I'll do whatever it takes to keep us right."

"I'm thinking he feels the same way."

Nat gave a half-shrug. "I know how lucky I am. And so are you."

Sofia sighed.

"Soph. Matt looks at you with undisguised adoration. You'll be fine. You can work through anything."

After drawing in a deep breath, Sofia asked, "Can you do me a favor?"

"Anything."

"Go to the restaurant with Gio and let me talk to Matt at your place. We'll catch up with you."

"Abso." She pulled out her phone, bent her head, and started texting. A minute later her phone pinged. "We're good. Gio is meeting me at Tallulah's Taqueria. We'll be sitting out back waiting for you guys." She pulled her keys out of her pocket. "Here." She gave Sofia walking directions back to the apartment, then headed in the other direction.

Five minutes later, Gio crossed the street to give Sofia a quick hug. "He's a good guy, Soph. It'll be all right." He hugged her tight, then went down the street.

She fumbled the keys so bad, Matt heard and opened the door. "Hey," he said as he stuffed his hands in his front pockets.

"Hey," she replied as she walked past him into the apartment.

He followed and she felt him standing behind her. Nat's words rang in Sofia's ears and she turned to face him. He was pulling his hands out of his pockets and before she knew what he intended, he muttered, "Fuck it," reached out and pulled her into his body as he leaned down and kissed her.

Ho-lee shit. No kiss ever felt like this.

His lips were soft and lush as they pressed against hers while the tip of his tongue moved along the seam, not pressing for entry as much as tasting. She wanted that tongue and opened for him, touching the tip of hers to his, and that tiny contact lit up her world. She grabbed his shirt to keep her standing as he groaned then speared his tongue into her mouth. Sofia was lost in the taste of him as he deepened the kiss, his arm tightening around her back as he drank her in. The strength, power, and ferocity of his mouth moving on hers made her dizzy with yearning. When she reached for his belt buckle, he lifted his mouth and kissed her cheeks, her eyelids, and then her forehead as he gently took her hands in his.

"I couldn't wait another minute," he rasped.

"A-huh," was all she could manage.

"I'm sorry about earlier. I shouldn't have asked."

She shook her head more to clear her brain than as a response. "You can ask me whatever you want. It's up to me whether to answer and how." She squeezed his hands. "I went on the pill about a year ago as a precaution since I'd been dating."

He dipped his chin, but he didn't say anything. His caramel coffee eyes, however, were speaking volumes, and most of what they were saying was *I love you*.

"I'm all yours, Matt. You'll be my first and only."

"I'm all yours, Miff. You are my forever and always."

The Di Caro Residence
Sofia's Graduation/Birthday Party
Natalia

Nat stood between Gio and Ro, who were flanked by their parents, *Nonna*, and Amy, as the rest of the family, all seventy thousand of them, stood in the backyard watching Sofia lean into Matt while looking down at a sheet cake that stretched over three tables. The eighteen candles grouped together in the middle flickered in the summer breeze as the chorus of hundreds of voices was winding up the "Happy Birthday" song. Sofia bent, blew out all the candles, and everyone cheered. Then, as if it were their first kiss, which Nat knew it damn well wasn't, Matt leaned down and lightly touched his mouth to Sofia's lips. Everyone applauded except Don Alessandro. Natch.

When Matt and Sofia had found Gio and Nat at Tallulah's Taqueria, Sofia's lips were red and puffy, and Matt had his arm around her shoulders protectively, as if he was carrying a sign that warned, *She's Mine*. Gio laughed, Nat smiled, and they had great food before Sofia and Matt left to go north.

Since then, Sofia and Nat talked every day, and Nat knew this was the way it would always be between them: sisters of the soul, sharing their lives, and depending on each other in good times and bad. When Nat fell for Gio, she had no idea how much fuller she would feel. Her heart nearly burst every morning from the joy of waking up next to him, and over the course of the day, with texts and calls from Francesca, Ro, *Nonna,* and Sofia, Nat's heart expanded and swelled with the love of family.

Sofia touched Nat's arm. "You're zoning."

"Good day. Everyone's behaving themselves, great food, and lots of booze. No complaints."

"Standards we can live by."

Nat laughed. "When do you and Amy head out?"

"Tomorrow morning. Our flight leaves Logan around eleven."

Nat poked Sofia in the ribs. "When is Matt arriving?"

Sofia got this dreamy look on her face. "Saturday morning. His flight gets in around nine."

"How will you survive for two days?"

"I know, right?"

Nat pulled Sofia in for a hug. "Love you. So happy for you."

"Love you back."

***

Sofia

"What do you have in here, Miff? A dumbbell set?" Matteo heaved the suitcase into the trunk.

"Everything's in one suitcase. You should be commending me."

"I have a feeling when you open it, it's going to explode."

She put her hand on her hip. "Don't be that guy."

Amy came barreling out of the house, her backpack dangling from her arm. "Sorry. Sorry. I couldn't find my phone charger."

"We have to go *now*," Matt ordered.

Sofia had said good-bye to everyone in the kitchen over a way-too-early breakfast, and made them promise not to come to the door and do the *she's leaving* scene. That they'd complied amazed her.

Amy climbed in the back, Sofia settled in the passenger seat, and then Matt closed her door and rounded the hood. A few minutes later they cleared the gate at the end of the driveway, turned right, and headed for the interstate.

At Logan Airport, he gave her a quick kiss and said, "See you in forty-eight hours. Have fun, and be safe."

She smiled, gave him one last hug then went into the terminal rolling her enormous suitcase alongside. She turned around and saw him standing by the car watching her. She put her hand over her heart, and he did the same.

***

S: We landed.
M: How was the flight?
S: I don't know. I slept.
M: Great flight then.

S: I know you're at work & can't talk. I'll text when we're in the hotel.
M: K
S: We're here, and wow. This is some place. Real European elegant.
M: Looking forward to seeing it.
S: Less than two days.
M: 43 hours 32 minutes.

Montreal was a beautiful city full of old-world charm. After she and Amy unpacked – adjoining rooms to keep nosy Parkers from minding Sofia and Matt's business – they ate at Dandy and had a fantastic lunch. Amy had a buttermilk fried chicken sandwich on brioche with apple *rémoulade*, and Sofia had the Israeli falafel salad. Divine. After, they went to the *Musée d'Art Contemporain de Montréal*, where Sofia could have stayed for a week, but Amy cried museum brain after two hours. They left and made their way to *Notre-Dame-de-Bonsecours* Chapel, the oldest chapel in the city: a church built over the original, which had burned down almost a hundred years after being erected.

Amy'd had enough culture for one day, and was looking forward to alcohol consumption. When they got back to their rooms, a bouquet of fifty Ballet Blonde Sweetheart roses sat on the round table in the seating area of Sofia's room. When she let out a shriek, Amy came running in.

"What? What happened?" Amy stopped short when she saw the bouquet. "Holy shit. They're gorgeous. What does the card say?"

Sofia shook her head. She'd been so stunned by the bouquet, she hadn't read the card yet. Amy grabbed it from its holder and pushed it into Sofia's hand. She slipped her finger under the flap, pulled out a thick crème stock card, read what Matt wrote – his handwriting – and teared up.

"Out loud, Soph."

Sofia waved her hand in front of her face to keep from crying. "Reflected beauty. Mere hours, my love."

"Well, fuck." Amy plopped down on the sofa. "Your brother pants over Nat, and you've got Lord Byron inside the body of a hot Italian. Talk about setting the bar too high. I'll never find anyone who'll measure up."

Sofia grinned, put the card back in its envelope, went to her bag, and zipped the card inside her wallet. "Give yourself a minute, Ames. You haven't even begun college yet."

"Well, neither have you, and you've got your Mr. Wonderful all sewn up already."

Sofia sat next to Amy. "You don't plan these things, you know. They happen. Like fall out of the sky."

"Or show up in the back hallway of a pastry shop."

Sofia had to smile. While it was true that had been her and Matt's first *moment*, she had actually met him outside church a couple of days before. "Go to synagogue."

Amy shifted to face Sofia. "What? Are you crazy? My parents sent me to a Catholic girls high school to keep me away from guys. I know more about your religion than mine. And besides, you know I'm not religious."

"Neither am I. But Enzo and Valentina dragged me to church every Sunday, and a couple of days before the pastry shop, I met Matt outside of church."

"So what are you telling me?" Amy threw her hands up and looked at the ceiling. "You guys meeting and falling in love was divine intervention?"

Sofia laughed. "Such drama." She smacked Amy's thigh. "No. What I'm saying is, you never know where *he* is, and when you're going to meet him. But he's out there, and you're going to find him. I know it like I'm sitting here."

"Whatever," Amy huffed.

Sofia looked at her watch. Six-thirty. "Listen, I'm gonna call Matt. Most everyone's left the office by now and he can talk. After we'll go to dinner. 'Kay?"

Amy stood and walked through the connecting door, which they had agreed to leave open when it was only them staying in the rooms. Amy grabbed its edge and pulled it closed behind her, then closed the door in her room, giving Sofia the privacy she needed.

Thirty seconds later, Matt's unbelievably handsome face appeared, and he said, "Miff," his voice husky and low.

She wanted to tell him to leave now. That she didn't know if she could wait until Saturday morning. But she kept it together enough to whisper, "The flowers are beyond words."

"Wanted you to know I'm thinking of you."

Sofia smiled. She could tell he was choosing his words carefully. She guessed some of his colleagues were still in the office, but she couldn't see more than a bit of the credenza behind his desk. "As you Brits say, well done you."

"What did you do today?"

She gave him the rundown, gushing over the museum and the beauty of the chapel.

"I love your artistic eye. You make everything so vibrant."

She blushed, and she knew he saw it when he dipped his head and smiled. That compliment meant everything, and was so him. She couldn't believe she'd found someone who saw and appreciated who she was at her core. "Remember that when we argue about paint colors."

"We won't argue about paint colors, curtains, or anything in the house. You do what you want."

"Hey. I thought we were going to be partners."

"We are partners. And this partner wants his partner to be happy. As you Yanks say, knock yourself out."

Huh. What did she do with that? She decided being gracious was the way to go. Only time would tell if his sentiments matched his actions, but she had a feeling they would. "Okay, Mr. Obliging. I'll hold you to it."

"Much obliged."

"Snarky."

He winked. "Missing you and counting the hours."

God. She wished she could hold him. Kiss him. Show him with every inch of her body how much he meant to her. "See you here, Saturday morning."

She pressed her lips against the screen then clicked off.

***

By the time Sofia went to sleep Friday night, she was exhausted. Amy, the best BF in the whole entire world, had made sure of it. She knew Sofia was ready to jump out of her skin waiting to see Matt, so Amy had scheduled an action-packed day. She'd woken Sofia at eight, and had them out the door and eating amazing crepes for breakfast in *Café de Mercanti* in Old Montreal by nine-thirty. After stuffing their faces, they went to the Montreal Museum of Fine Arts, where Amy was a trooper and hung in for three hours. When she cried her feet hurt and she needed food, they left and went to Robin Square near the old port of Montreal. Sofia had the quiche – yum – and a small salad, and Amy had the mac and cheese, a staple in her diet. They were supposed to visit the Botanical Gardens, but a thunderstorm hit as they were finishing eating, and they decided to go to *Réso, La ville souterraine* – the underground city. Shopping.

Interestingly, Amy's feet didn't hurt anymore, and when Sofia checked her phone, they'd walked twenty thousand steps by the time they'd combed through more stores than she could count.

After they'd dumped their bags in their hotel rooms – they both bought way too much, but the shops were fabulous – they'd cleaned up, changed, and went out to eat, drink, and dance. Earlier, they'd passed a place near the museum, Thursdays, that had all three. At the bistro, Amy had the *Pernod* scallops, Sofia had the mushroom risotto, and since the drinking age in Montreal was eighteen, they'd each had a martini. Sofia was done after the first, but Amy knocked back two before she said the room was spinning. They went downstairs to the club and danced for a little more than an hour before they admitted to being wiped out. Sofia set her alarm for eight in the morning so she could be ready for Matt, who was due to arrive at the hotel at nine-thirty.

A minute before midnight she'd fallen into bed, and was out the moment her head hit the pillow.

***

Matteo

Matteo sat in the corner wing chair eyeing the shopping bags scattered around the floor of Sofia's hotel room. His girl loved to shop. He smiled, remembering how minutes before running into her in the back hallway of the *pasticceria*, she'd been shopping in Vittoria.

He heard the water go off in the shower and waited for her to come out, trying to remain as still as possible. The bathroom door opened, and she walked past him, a towel wrapped around her slim body, and one done up turban-style on her head. She was muttering under her breath.

"Where'd I put you? Where are you? Dammit." She turned to survey the room and did a double take when her gaze fell on him. "Ohmygod," she screeched, then launched herself at him. He put out his arms in time to catch her before she slammed into him. "What...why...who cares." She shoved her knees between the outside of his thighs and the chair's arms, lowered her bare ass – god help him not to come in his jeans – and leaned in to lay her soft, plump lips on his.

He gave her a few moments before he took over the kiss, rubbing their lips together. He took advantage of her sigh and pushed his tongue into her mouth, the remains of toothpaste flavoring her natural sweet taste. When her tongue touched his, he could no longer contain the fire that had been burning in his body. He stood, her legs went around his waist, and he walked her to the bed where the sheets were disheveled from her sleep. Gently, he laid her down and placed his hands on her cheeks.

"My Sofia." His thumbs brushed her brows as his gaze wandered her delicate features. "So beautiful." Her smile made her lovely blue eyes tilt up, and the apple of her cheeks reddened. "All mine." He moved his hands down her throat and to her shoulders, where the skin was like silk. Soft and smooth: a masterpiece of anatomy. When his fingers brushed the top of the towel, he asked, "May I?" and she nodded, the smile never leaving her face.

Slowly, he pulled at the tucked piece until the towel fell away, leaving her bare before him. He'd known she was small boned, and had seen her in a one-piece bathing suit, but he hadn't been prepared for what lay before him. A perfect woman's body proportioned to her tiny frame. Her breasts were small and high with garnet nipples hard and ready for his mouth. Her waist was nipped in, and the flare of her small hips was graceful. He'd seen her slender thighs, which managed to barely touch directly below her perfect pussy. Old Sicilian men joked that women whose thighs didn't touch were bad lays, and although he gave no credence to the gossip of ancients, he loved that were such tales true, his Sofia wouldn't be afflicted.

"You are magnificent, *cara*." A flush suffused her body, the red spreading across her chest, up her throat, and to her still smiling face.

He pulled the towel out from under her and rested his hands on her thighs. "I'm so hungry for you, I don't know where to begin."

She held out her arms and wiggled her fingers. He leaned into his hands, holding his weight off her as he bent his head and began to swirl his tongue across one delicious nipple.

"Dear god," she moaned and began to writhe beneath him.

He sucked the nipple into his mouth and bit down lightly. Her responsive body bowed, her hips hitting his, making his cock strain even harder to get where he wanted it to be. He moved his hands to her back, pulling her up to him as he moved his mouth to her other breast to taste, lick, suck, and nibble. The towel around her head fell away, which seemed to bring her back to the moment. She looked at him. Her pupils were blown. She was already there, in that space where need controlled her every desire.

Happy to join her over the edge, he knew when he wasn't shaking with want, he would spend some serious time feasting on her delectable breasts. But for now, he needed to make sure she was truly ready for him, and that he took care of her. Once he was inside her, he knew he wouldn't last. Not the first time. And given her virginity, he wouldn't be going in for rounds two, three, and four until tomorrow, when she wasn't sore.

Matteo trailed his tongue down the center of her torso, lowering his head as he brushed his face in the soft curls above her pussy. He shifted his hands to her hips, and moving her slight body was the work of a moment. Her legs were dangling over the edge of the bed, and he knelt between them. Without a prompt, she threw her legs over his shoulders, and raised herself onto her elbows, watching as he dipped his head between her thighs. He held her gaze as he ran his tongue through her folds, but when the taste of her hit his mouth, his focus shifted to the bounty at his lips. Sweet and tangy, like the ripest blood orange, he became instantly addicted to her. The lust that had been riding him now cracked him wide open. Everything, absolutely everything about his Sofia was made for him, and him alone. And he planned on feasting with abandon.

His tongue was inside her as his thumb pressed and released her engorged clit while his other hand pressed on her belly to keep her from flying off the bed. No surprise, she was wild, fierce, and communicative. Every time he did something she liked, she screamed, "More." When he changed tactics to something she didn't like, she cried out, "No. Go back to what you were doing."

As tiny as she was, he could barely contain her thrashing as she chased her climax. Now, working her relentlessly, she was close and began chanting his name. When he squeezed her clit with his thumb and forefinger, she clenched her legs around his neck and her internal muscles gripped his tongue while she near levitated off the bed. Then she began to scream, "You gotta stop. I can't take any more." He wanted to wring another orgasm out of her, but decided, this first time, he wouldn't push her limits. But damn. Nothing about their sex was going to be delicate and controlled. Matteo had discovered he'd fallen for a tornado in a bottle.

He rubbed her thighs and she took the hint and unwrapped her legs, allowing him to stand. When he got a look at her flushed face wearing a grin that broadcasted satisfied in capital letters, he wanted to pound his chest. Before he had the chance to go all he-man, she flicked her wrist and told him, "Take off your clothes so I can torture you now." She moved up the bed and leaned against the headboard while stuffing pillows behind her back.

A quick study, his Sofia. He grinned and removed his clothes slowly, giving her what she wanted, but treating her to the thrill of anticipation. She'd seen him in swim trunks, but that didn't stop her from licking her lips when his shirt fell to the floor, baring his chest. "You like what you see, *cara*?"

"I like that it's mine."

"Greedy."

"Unabashedly." She stretched her legs out in front of her, crossing them at the ankles. "Carry on," she cooed.

Oh yeah. He was going to enjoy a lifetime of being enthralled by this tiny enchantress.

He stepped out of his shoes, toed off his socks, and undid his belt. Then he stepped to the side of the bed and asked, "Care to help?"

She grinned, got on all fours, and prowled to the edge of the mattress then sat on her feet as she unbuttoned his jeans, then pulled down the zipper slowly, for which he was grateful since his engorged cock was pressing mercilessly against the steel teeth. When the sides fell open, she rose to her knees and began to kiss his belly while sliding one hand inside his briefs. Maintaining control caused the muscles in his calves to clench as her slim, soft fingers brushed the head of his dick. Unable to remain standing if this continued, he shoved his hands inside his briefs and pushed them down with his jeans. His hands went around her torso as he stepped out of his pants and fell onto the bed, taking her down with him.

"I'm not finished," she told him as she put her hands on his chest and pushed him back as she threw a leg over his body and then rested her ass on his thighs. "My, my," she teased. "Everything about you is big and thick." No more teasing, she wrapped her hand around his cock and it took every ounce of concentration to keep from coming. "You're so hard, but the skin is so soft and smooth." She rubbed her thumb across the head of his cock, catching the bead of come and smoothing it over and under as she trailed her finger down to his balls. She cupped him and squeezed gently.

That did it. He jackknifed up, growled, "Sofia," and flipped her as he moved between her legs, spreading her thighs with his hips. The head of his dick lay against her entrance and he wanted in so badly he almost lost himself to the temptation of her sweet, tight pussy. "I'm big," he rasped.

"I saw," she whispered in his ear then bit his lobe.

"I don't want to hurt you."

"You won't."

He drew in a deep breath. "You have to tell me if you need me to stop." When she didn't answer, he rested his forehead against hers. "Miff. You have to talk to me if it's too much." He felt her nod.

He moved his hand between them and ran his fingers through her slick folds. Wet and ready, she shifted her legs to entwine with his, and gently, he began to stroke her clit as he inched his way inside her. She was so tight and felt so small beneath him. "You all right?"

"Mmmm hmmm." She lifted her pelvis, sliding him in deeper until he felt it, the barrier between innocence and carnality.

With one thrust, he seated himself deep within her and held still. She wrapped her arms around his neck and whispered, "Now and forever, I'm all yours."

Part of him wanted to pound into her with wanton abandon, and part of him wanted to gather her in his arms and stay exactly as they were: joined. But desire had bitten his Sofia and she began to move beneath him, and his body was happy to join the party. Slowly, he pulled out a little and thrust back in.

"Do that again," she breathed into his ear.

He did, and the next time he pulled out a little farther, and thrust in a little harder.

"Mmmm. That feels divine. More."

With one hand beneath her tiny tight ass, and the other between them working her clit, he rocked in her, keeping a steady pace as her breathing sped up and the noises she made became more urgent.

"Matt. Matt," she chanted, and he knew he wouldn't let himself go until she went with him. He thrust faster and deeper and as she dug her nails into his shoulders, the walls of her tight channel grabbed his cock. "Matt," she screamed as he exploded inside her, the intensity of his orgasm catching his breath in his throat as his heart pounded against his ribcage.

He moved the hand between them and put his elbow on the mattress to keep his full weight off her. He stroked her hair, tucking it behind her ear as he watched her face relax and her beautiful blue eyes open to catch his.

"You're really good at that," she murmured.

He smiled and touched his lips to hers. "You okay?"

"Never been better." She reached up and traced his brow with her fingers. "I'm glad you got here early, but you must be tired. You want to take a nap?"

Sofia wasn't coy, but Matteo had a feeling she was speaking in code. "I wouldn't mind a cuddle," he said. She nuzzled his neck. "Relax, Miff. I'm going to pull out." He felt her body go limp, and slowly, and reluctantly, he left her sweet, tight body. "Wait right there." He went to the bathroom, cleaned up, and brought a hot towel back with him. "Here. Let's take care of you." Which he did, then tossed the towel to floor, yanked up the bedclothes and gathered his Sofia against his chest. "Sleep, my love."

Matteo held Sofia while she slept, and eventually, he dozed off, his heart never having felt so full.

***

He woke first, and went to the bathroom to draw a hot bath to help ease Sofia's muscles. Naked, she shuffled in as he was turning off the faucets.

"I'm not a bath person," she squeezed out between a yawn and a stretch.

"Typically, I'm not either, but you should soak a bit. It'll help keep you from getting too sore."

She shrugged. "Okay. Come in with me?"

He nodded, slid into the tub, and held out his arm for her to lean on as she climbed in, snugging her bottom against his groin. It took all of ten seconds for his cock to get hard. "Ignore that," he said, and she laughed.

"What if I don't want to?"

"Starting tomorrow, I don't want you to for the rest of our lives, but today, let's take it slow."

"I haven't returned the favor yet."

He dipped his head and turned hers by her chin so he could see her face. "You most certainly have."

"Nuh-uh. You went down on me, and I want to go down on you."

Good Christ. She was going to kill him. "Later, Miff."

"Okay."

She'd agreed too quickly, and when they were out of the tub, and he'd finished rubbing her down with the fluffy bath towel, she dropped to her knees on the bathmat, wrapped her hand around the root of his dick, and began licking at the head as she fondled his balls. When her mouth sucked him in, he slapped one hand onto the wall, sifted his fingers into her hair, and held on to her head with his other hand. He didn't guide her, and he didn't pump into her mouth: he let her work him, and damn, she was a natural.

When he was close, he tried to pull out, but she wouldn't let go, and she squeezed his balls just enough to send him over the edge. He groaned as he came, and she swallowed every last drop. He'd been prepared to wait a while to do this until she got comfortable with their intimacy, but Sofia didn't need to ease into their physical relationship. All in and thrilled to be there, she looked like a fairy princess, but was a bawdy tart at heart.

Matteo couldn't believe his good fortune.

***

They'd met Amy for a late lunch, walked the old city and stopped at a few attractions, then had dinner at Stash Café where they overindulged in *pierogi*. Sunday, Sofia wore him out in the best possible way.

She woke him by grabbing his morning hard-on and asked, "Is this an every morning occurrence?" He nodded. "Oh, I'm going to enjoy waking up."

He grinned. "Me too."

Only room service and a late morning nap broke up the marathon of shower sex, sofa sex, against-the-wall sex, oral sex, and four-positions-in-bed sex. They'd stayed naked and sweaty most of the day, and when Matteo got dressed to leave for the airport, Sofia pulled on a pair of jeans and a t-shirt to walk him to the lobby.

He held her close in the elevator and whispered in her ear, "Next weekend in Toronto, Miff."

"I know I sound whiny, but I hate that I can't sleep next to you every night."

"Soon, my love. You enjoy this adventure and milk it for all it's worth. You're not going to have this kind of freedom again."

"If you say so."

"I know so."

On the sidewalk, in front of a waiting taxi, Matteo kissed his Sofia deeply. "Go inside, Miff."

She nodded. "Call me when you get home."

"I promise." Then he got in the cab and went back to Boston, knowing his heart would be wherever Sofia travelled.

Boston, Back Bay
Matteo's Home
Sofia

Sofia was in her office. The office Matt had given her free hand to decorate to make her own. He hadn't been kidding when he told her she could do whatever she wanted. He didn't care, as long as she was happy.

She'd left happy behind somewhere in Canada, and moved through ecstatic and elated to I-can't-believe-he's-for-real. As promised, he'd called when he got home from Montreal, and each weekend he met her wherever Amy and Sofia had travelled. He'd shown her the hedonistic side of sex, where anything they wanted to do to each other was safe and allowed. By the end of their last weekend, she knew his body as well as she did her own, and had learned the meaning of erotic.

After she and Amy returned to Connecticut, Amy went home, packed up everything she owned, then hightailed it to Boston. Sofia had spent one week in her parents' home, allowing her family to fawn all over her before she left for college.

Following Nat's advice, Sofia let her family take her to Tufts, where they got her settled in her dorm, met her roommate, and walked the campus before taking off. Sofia had listened carefully to what Nat had said, and bought a second cell phone, leaving her "family" phone under her mattress in the dorm when she left to go to Matteo's home, where she slept every night.

Life was as close to perfect as it could get. Her classes were hard, but exactly what she wanted. Her art was the focus of her education, and the balm her soul needed when school stressed her out.

Matt was a gift. The best man she knew, and most days, she couldn't believe he was hers. Yes, they fought. Not like Gio and Nat, thank God, but there were times Sofia found herself grinding her teeth.

Matt was patient and rational, which made her crazy when she wanted him to yell back. Most of the time he let her blow out her mad then brought her back to center. Occasionally, he got pissed off, but he was careful not to say things he couldn't un-say, and mostly, he was so thrilled they were together, he didn't get thrown off track. His goal in life was for them to have a long and happy life together, surrounded by their family. Little did he know, he was going to get his wish sooner than he thought.

"How did this happen?" Sofia waited for her new ob-gyn to answer. "And don't tell me the usual way. I've taken my pills every day."

"Did you take them at the same time every day?"

Well, shit. "No. When I moved, everything got thrown off until I got settled, and for about a week, I took them at different times during the day, sometimes at night."

"That'd do it. With some people, if their hormone levels are maintained rigidly, the pills' effectiveness can be diluted."

I bet it doesn't help that we fuck like rabbits, and Matt's one potent dude with unending stamina.

"Is there any…do I have to worry about birth defects because I kept taking the pill after I got pregnant?"

"The pill you took had hormones that prevented ovulation. Since that occurred and the egg was fertilized, the pill's purpose was obviated. Can I say with one hundred percent certainty there won't be a problem with the fetus? No. But there are many factors to consider, and taking the pill past conception is low on my list of concerns."

Holy shit. Sofia was shaking. "Do you have others?"

"No. You're young and healthy. Unless you tell me about symptoms you're experiencing outside typical changes your body will be going through, I'm guessing we'll see each other at our regularly scheduled visits, and you'll deliver a healthy baby."

That sounded better. "Okay. All right. Thanks for calling me back. I've been freaking out over here."

The doctor chuckled. "Call if you need me. I'll see you in about three weeks."

Sofia put the phone on her drafting table and envisioned Matt's face when she told him. Which would be happening in about three minutes. She heard the code pad beeping.

"Miff," he called from the front hall.

"In my office," she answered.

He came through the door, took one look at her face, and stopped. "What happened?"

Ninety-nine percent of the time, she loved that he read her so well. Today, she could've done with a reprieve as she gathered her thoughts.

She walked over to him, put her arms around his waist and he hugged her close, his arms encircling her. "Change of plans," she murmured.

He pulled back a little and his brow furrowed as he looked down at her. "Can you be more specific?"

She wanted to laugh. Calm and rational were about to fly out the fucking window. "Ah...yeah. I'm pregnant."

He blinked. Then blinked again. Then a slow smile creased his exquisite face. "Unexpected. A tad earlier than we'd planned, but certainly happy news."

She stepped back and crossed her arms over her chest. "How the fuck can you be so calm?"

"Well, let's break this down, shall we? Do you love me?"

She rolled her eyes. "Do you have to ask?"

"Humor me."

"Of course I love you."

"Excellent news since I love you too. Do you plan to spend the rest of your life with me?"

She wanted to smack him right now. "If twenty questions continues, I'm rethinking my position on that answer."

He laughed, and he looked so good doing it, she couldn't stay angry with him. "Come here." She walked into his open arms. "We talked about getting married in a couple of years, and starting a family when you graduated. I would have loved for you to have that time for yourself, but we're going to be parents in..."

"Early summer."

"So, we'll move up the marriage date as we get ready for our first little Parisi sooner than planned. The only thing that changes is timing. We'll get help in so you can resume classes next fall, and I'll arrange some parental leave time to make sure one of us is around as much as we can be. I have no doubt your grandmother and mother will be more than happy to help out. We'll be fine, Miff. As long as we have each other, we'll be better than fine."

She sighed. His strength, constant and never-ending patience, his devotion were the kind of things she'd hoped for in her life partner, but to have found them felt like a miracle. "I'm so lucky to have you."

"And here I was thinking how lucky I am to have you."

She looked up at him and smiled. "Okay, hotshot. How you want to do this marriage thing?"

"Small."

Now she laughed. "How small?"

"Your parents, *Nonna*, Gio, Nat, Ro, Amy, and my dad, if he's well enough to travel."

"One more. Theresa."

"Of course. Theresa." He stepped back and took her hand. "Let's do a little research."

Massachusetts had a three-day waiting period, and getting the license was easy. Finding a church and priest to perform the marriage in Boston? Piece of cake. They'd booked the wedding for two Saturdays from tomorrow. Sofia didn't want a poofy foo-foo wedding gown. She wanted something elegant and off the rack. Matteo decided to buy a new suit. No morning coat or tux. They called their favorite restaurant in North Beach and booked a table for eleven in the back room for Saturday evening, two weeks from tomorrow.

They asked Amy to come over for dinner tomorrow night to coincide with Gio and Nat's arrival. Sofia and Matteo needed a game plan to tell her parents, and decided they needed to marshal their defenses.

"You know," she said from her favorite post-sex position, sprawled naked across Matt's chest, "I'm half inclined to call my Aunt Toni for advice since she sort of lived this with my father."

"What's the down side of calling her?"

"She'll want to come to the wedding, which will mean all her brood will come, and then all of her siblings and their broods will want to come. If that weren't enough, once my mother's side of the family finds out my father's side of the family is coming, all hell will break loose, and we'll have a guest list of six hundred people."

"Don't you dare call your Aunt Toni."

She grinned. "Agreed."

***

Turned out, all those years as *Nonna*'s kitchen helper meant Sofia knew how to cook. She made garlic bread – she didn't make the bread from scratch, not when there were three great bakeries within walking distance of their house – a huge salad, vegetable lasagna – she made the sauce from scratch – and they bought *cannoli* from North Beach, because everyone knew the best *cannoli* came from North Beach.

The table was set, and the wine was decanted. The baked stuffed mushrooms were out on the coffee table in the living room, and Matt had cued up his playlist and they were listening to classic Motown.

Amy arrived first, took in the food, the wine, and the music and said, "Holy shit. This is serious."

Nat and Gio arrived a few minutes later, took one look at Sofia, and said in tandem, "Pregnant."

Sofia glanced down at her flat stomach and asked, "How'd you know?"

Her brother answered, "We had a three-hour car ride up here to work it out, but we agreed your face would give you away."

She smacked his arm. "What's wrong with my face?"

"Nothing, Soph. You look happy." She gave him bug eyes.

"What he's trying to say," Nat jumped in, "is that if it were bad news we'd be able to tell if you had been crying or were upset. Since it's happy news, there were only a few choices that would require us to hear the news in person."

Amy stared at Sofia. "You're pregnant?"

"Affirmative."

"What the fuck? You're on the pill."

"Affirmative again, but when I moved and started school, I was thrown off and didn't take the pills at the same time every day. My hormonal levels dropped and –"

Gio cut her off. "Italian super sperm got the job done."

Nat smacked him on the arm.

"What?" He grinned at Matt. "Dude's got –"

"Ahem," Nat interrupted, shaking her head. "Not cool, my man."

Gio looked at Nat. "Ace," he crooned then winked. He turned to Sofia. "C'mere. Lemme give you a hug." Sofia walked into Gio's embrace. "Anything you need, we're here for you, baby sister."

"Thanks." Then she whispered, "I don't think you're wrong about the Italian super sperm thing." Gio cracked up.

Dinner became the strategy session Sofia had hoped for.

"Straight on, man. I'm telling you. Best way to deal with my dad. Like ripping off a bandage. Hurts like a mother for a moment, then it's over and you can move on."

Matt cleared his throat. "There's an underlying issue between your father and me." Everyone stared at Matt, and Sofia leaned forward to put her hand over his. "My family was experiencing some difficulties after my brothers died, and your father thought it best to keep Sofia out of the fray. I agreed and promised not to contact her. I broke that promise when we started writing to each other, and, as you know, your father found out." Amy ducked her head. "I don't see how this most recent development will imbue good faith and more trust. In other words, straight on might not be the best course."

Silence hung, then Nat put down her fork. "Even if he's pissed off, what are his choices? He'd never hang Soph out to dry, and he'd never hurt you. He knows she'd hate him forever if he did. He's smart, and he knows she's holding the ultimate weapon." She motioned to Sofia's stomach. "His grandchild."

"*Nonna*'s great-grandchild," Amy added. "Listen, it doesn't matter if how and when you got knocked up wasn't kosher." She grinned at Sofia. "The end result is you're marrying a nice Italian Catholic guy who has bank, a good job, and he loves you."

"Yeah, well, tell that to Aunt Toni," Sofia said.

"She's right about that." Gio poured Nat and himself another glass of wine, and tilted the bottle toward Amy, who passed her glass to him. "But I think this'll be different. Dad didn't know Aaron from a hole in the wall, and he showed up married to Dad's baby sister who was," he motioned a curve over his stomach, "preggers. He knows Matt, and let's be real. Someone has been keeping tabs up here."

"Ugh," Sofia groaned.

"C'mon, Soph. You gotta know that's true."

Sofia sighed. "Yeah. But I try not to think about it."

"Gio's been watched since he started at Brown." Nat shrugged. "Someone's still on us. Both of us. Every now and again, I feel someone watching. You better than me know it's part of being in this family."

"Right." Matt stood. "Since he knows you're here," he flipped his hand toward Gio, Nat, and Amy, "let's make it official." He walked into the kitchen and came back with his phone.

"What are you doing?" Sofia shrieked.

"Calling him and asking him, Francesca, Ro, and *Nonna* to come up tomorrow. We'll lay out a traditional Sunday meal." Sofia's mouth fell open. "Don't worry, *cara*." He kissed her nose. "We'll pick up the food. You're not cooking for nine people."

"I could." She defended her skills.

"No doubt." He smiled. "But not on such short notice."

Matt touched his phone screen a couple of times then sat down as he said, "Good evening, Don. I hope it's not too late to call."

"Brown nose," Gio mouthed.

"Everything is fine, sir. Sofia and I wondered if you, *Donna* Di Caro, Aurora, and *Nonna* are available tomorrow to come up for Sunday dinner."

"Two would be perfect. See you tomorrow." Matt touched the screen and put down the phone. "Oh yeah. He knows you're all here."

"Well, shit."

***

Gio and Nat slept in the guest bedroom, and Amy slept in Matt's office on the sofa's pullout bed. Everyone stumbled into the kitchen around eight-thirty, wearing last night's three bottles of wine. Except Sofia, whose happy morning vibe seemed to annoy Amy and Gio the most.

"Don't you have to vomit or something?" Amy complained as she poured a huge mug of coffee.

"Nope," Sofia chirped on purpose. "No morning sickness."

"Why...how did you know you were pregnant?" Amy sank into a kitchen chair.

"I didn't. I went to the doctor for a birth control prescription. Since we're new to each other, she did the annual exam, and told me she thought I was pregnant, but pulled blood to make sure, and to check for anything else it might've been."

"Huh." Amy took a long sip of coffee then said, "Ahh. That's better." Then she seemed to wait until her brain kicked in. "So, how far along are you?"

"About nine weeks."

"That'll make Thanksgiving dinner interesting." Gio held out his mug toward her belly. "You think you'll be showing in three weeks?"

"Since I'm new at this, I'm not sure, but I'm guessing not really."

"You're tiny," Gio said. "I bet you'll have a bump by then."

Sofia turned to Matt. "Let's go away for Thanksgiving. I don't want to face fifty members of my family so soon."

"Sure." He shrugged. "We'll call it our honeymoon. Where do you want to go?"

She grinned. "Montreal."

***

Matt and Gio had gone to North Beach to pick up the feast they ordered while Nat and Amy went to the bakery, the florist, and the green grocer. By two o'clock the house was festooned with fresh flowers, smelled of garlic bread and Italian food, which was being kept warm in the double ovens.

When the downstairs buzzer rang, Matt squeezed her hand and said, "I'll get it, Miff. Take a deep breath, baby." She nodded, and as she watched him walk down the hall looking purposeful, she realized, except for Gio and Nat, her family hadn't been here before.

A few minutes later she heard:

"How lovely." Mom.

"*Elegante.*" *Nonna.*

"Fresh." Ro.

"Matteo." Dad. Who didn't sound anywhere near sanguine.

Gio and Nat, who had been sitting on one of the sofas, stood when everyone came into the room. Hugs and kisses all around, and Mom's exclamation, "Why, Amy. I didn't know you were here, honey."

"Hey, Mrs. D. Yeah, well, I live close by and Sofia takes pity on me and feeds me every once in a while."

Nonna nodded. "Sofia's a good girl."

Nat had to hide her grin, and Sofia nearly choked.

"Want a tour?" Sofia offered, knowing *Nonna* couldn't wait to stick her nose into every corner of the place. As Mom, Ro, and *Nonna* traipsed behind Sofia, she heard Matt offer her father a whiskey. He better take it. He was going to need it.

Dinner went off without a hitch. Even *Nonna* had to allow the food was "decent," which meant really good, but she'd never compliment anyone else's cooking. Sofia, Amy, Nat, and Gio told college-related stories, and Matt shared his most recent work project. Even though the meal went smoothly, everyone was politely waiting for the other shoe to fall. Even Ro held her tongue.

Matt sat at the head of the table, Sofia's father at the other end, which was bold of Matt, but made a statement: his home, his table. After coffee and dessert, Matt cleared his throat and looked Dad right in the eye. "We're happy you could join us to share in our happy news." Jesus. How could he be so smooth and composed? Sofia's stomach was in knots. "We're getting married in a couple of weeks," Mom gasped, "which is sooner than we had planned, but we're expecting our first child this summer, and we didn't want to wait."

Dad's lips thinned, Mom put her hands over her heart, and *Nonna* got up and came straight to Sofia, who was pulled up and into a fierce hug. In Italian *Nonna* said, "Thank you for making it possible for me to meet my great-grandchild. You'll be a wonderful mother."

Sofia hugged *Nonna* tightly and whispered in her ear, "You'll come up and help me?"

"Any time you want, my precious girl."

As *Nonna* moved away, Mom was right there, tears streaming down her cheeks. "I'm good, Mom," Sofia assured her mother. "Happy. Not what we had planned, but we'll make it work."

"I know you will, sweetheart. I'm here for you."

Sofia hugged her mother and said, "I'm counting on it."

Which left Dad, who'd remained seated, glaring at Matt. "You know what I expected," Dad ground out.

"Sofia plans to stay in school, sir. We will bring in help, and I'll adjust my schedule."

Dad said nothing but nodded once, which in Don Alessandro speak meant, *Okay, we'll see.*

"With respect, and I know this is a lot coming at you with short notice, but we want a small wedding. Everyone who is here, plus Theresa and my father." Dad narrowed his eyes. Sofia could hear him counting how many more men he'd need to bring in to beef up security. "We're going to take a short honeymoon over Thanksgiving. Sofia has already given notice to Tufts that she's vacating her dorm room." Sofia's roommate wouldn't be happy come January. She'd have a full-fledged occupant next semester.

Matt continued running it down for Dad, "We've made arrangements to have a wedding dinner at our favorite restaurant in North Beach." More eye narrowing while Dad surely was working out how to vett (read: put the fear of God into) the restaurant owners and staff.

Gio stood, breaking the tension and putting a period at the end of the hostilities. "I say this calls for a toast." Sofia so loved her brother.

Nat and Amy brought out the champagne flutes, and Gio popped the cork and poured. Last, he gave Sofia barely a sip's worth, put down the bottle then turned to face her and Matt, who had his arm draped over her shoulder.

"To my sister and my new brother. Congrats." He held out his hand and Nat linked her fingers with his. "We wish you a happy, healthy, long life filled with love and laughter."

Sofia teared up as she raised her glass to clink against Matt's. Before she could take her tiny sip, Matt lowered his head and gave her a sweet kiss with a little tongue and a promise for later. "I love you," she whispered.

"Forever, my love," he returned.

Boston, Back Bay
Parisi Home
Matteo

"Take the car, Miff. I'll leave it for you." They'd had this conversation before, but that was three months ago when his wife wasn't pregnant, there wasn't hard snow on the ground, and ice everywhere.

"There's nowhere to park. They tell everyone to take mass transit."

The outside buzzer rang, and he checked the dedicated iPad on the kitchen wall to see who was downstairs trying to come up. Another deliveryman. Since Francesca had sent out post-wedding announcements, a steady stream of high-end gifts had been arriving, along with sizeable checks. No one wanted to disappoint Don Alessandro, and no one in the family wanted to be outdone. Matteo and Sofia's home was overrun with boxes affixed with colour-coded sticky notes: from whom; keeping it; not sure; return; and thank you note sent. Sofia had made Nat promise to head off any attempts at a baby shower, but even with Nat at the helm, that request did not hold much promise it would be honoured.

"Then take a Lyft. It's better," he called as he buzzed in the deliveryman.

"No." Her voice was right behind him so he turned to face her. "It's better to walk if it's nice out, and take the bus or the train if it's not."

Stubborn. The more pregnant she looked – and that little bump was sweet – the more she fought him on any and everything. Only once she admitted to never giving up the ground she'd gained over the past six months. His Sofia had become an independence warrior. "You have to walk to get to the bus or the train."

"Like two blocks," she lied.

"Try six. Take a Lyft, Miff."

The doorbell rang and Matteo checked the iPad again to make sure it was the same deliveryman at their front door. Matteo walked down the hallway, opened the door, accepted the huge box, put it on the floor behind him, signed the handheld device then closed and locked the door.

Sofia was standing in the hallway with her hands on her hips, which was never a good sign. "Are you telling me?"

He'd learned quickly the inflections in her tone and the vagaries of her nose twitch. "Well, no. I'm expressing my opinion."

"When I get the British answer, I know it's bullshit."

He reined in his sigh. "Why are we arguing about this?"

"Because *Nonna* told Nat that whatever she allows Gio to do in their first month of marriage, she should be prepared to put up with their entire marriage."

Matteo always thrilled at Sofia's casual acceptance of their forever-ness, but right now he had a bone to pick with *Nonna*. "I'm not trying to get away with anything here. I'm looking out for you. You're pregnant. It's called caring."

"Now I'm getting the snotty response." She crossed her slender arms over her chest, having no idea what a pretty picture she made even in her pique.

Lovely all the time, he enjoyed when she was riled up. Call him stupid, but he loved when she let loose her fire. From the start, he'd known she wouldn't be easy to live with, yet, oft times, he stoked the flame, enjoying her stamping out her independence, as if he had any intention of robbing her of the thing she treasured most. "Compromise?"

"Let's hear it, not-the-boss-of-me."

He looked down at his trainers to keep from chuckling, then recaptured her gaze. "Walk and mass transit only if the weather is nice, and there's no snow or ice on the ground. Lyft when there's snow, ice, below freezing weather, and rain." He knew her well enough to spell things out, or she'd find a loophole and exploit it.

She regarded him as if there was a punchline she was missing. "I can do that."

Now he sighed audibly. "Thank Christ." Then he reached out, grabbed her wrist, and pulled her to him. Instantly, her arms wound around his waist. "Isn't this better?"

"Yeah. But it's a fuck of a lotta work to get here."

He threw his head back and let loose, knowing his life would be filled with love, joy, laughter, and the constant bone-deep pleasure of having this feisty woman at his side forevermore.

ABOUT THE AUTHOR

Elle Wright has been writing stories since she was a child, which led her to a career in journalism. She enjoys reporting life as much as making up a world she can control. She lives on the east coast of the United States where most of her large, noisy family resides. When she isn't in front of her computer, she loves to travel, garden, hang out with her dogs, and take in the brisk sea air that she's told is supposed to help calm her. She's been testing that theory for a while now.

CONNECT WITH ELLE:
Twitter: @ElleWright18
Instagram: @Elle_Wright_Writes
FB: facebook.com/elle.wright.1460

www.BOROUGHSPUBLISHINGGROUP.com

If you enjoyed this book, please write a review. Our authors appreciate the feedback, and it helps future readers find books they love. We welcome your comments and invite you to send them to info@boroughspublishinggroup.com. Follow us on Facebook, Twitter and Instagram, and be sure to sign up for our newsletter for surprises and new releases from your favorite authors.

Are you an aspiring writer? Check out www.boroughspublishinggroup.com/submit and see if we can help you make your dreams come true.

www.ingramcontent.com/pod-product-compliance
Lightning Source LLC
Chambersburg PA
CBHW031352170626
46807CB00002B/934